Night

OF THE

Fireflies

SummerHill Secrets

❧   ❧

Whispers Down the Lane
Secret in the Willows
Catch a Falling Star
Night of the Fireflies
A Cry in the Dark
House of Secrets
Echoes in the Wind
Hide Behind the Moon
Windows on the Hill
Shadows Beyond the Gate

NIGHT
OF THE
FIREFLIES

Beverly Lewis

BETHANY HOUSE PUBLISHERS
MINNEAPOLIS, MINNESOTA 55438

Night of the Fireflies
Copyright © 1995
Beverly Lewis

Cover illustration by Chris Ellison

Published by Bethany House Publishers
A Ministry of Bethany Fellowship International
11400 Hampshire Avenue South
Minneapolis, Minnesota 55438
www.bethanyhouse.com

Printed in the United States of America by
Bethany Press International, Minneapolis, Minnesota 55438

Library of Congress Cataloging-in-Publication Data

Lewis, Beverly, 1949–
    Night of the fireflies / Beverly Lewis.
        p.   cm. — (SummerHill secrets ; 4)
    Summary: When a car strikes her young Amish friend while the two
of them catch fireflies, thirteen-year-old Merry hopes for healing
through her Christian faith.
    ISBN 1–55661–479–9
    [1. Amish—Fiction. 2. Christian life—Fiction. 3. Fireflies—
Fiction.] I. Title. II. Series: Lewis, Beverly, 1949–
SummerHill secrets ; 42.
PZ7.L58464Ni   1995
[Fic]—dc20   95–43838
                                                              CIP
                                                               AC

For
Mother and Dad,
who caught lightning bugs
in Pennsylvania
and Kansas
long before they met.

Now . . .
they catch souls for the Kingdom.
Together.

BEVERLY LEWIS is a speaker, teacher, and the best-selling author of the HOLLY'S HEART series. She has written more than twenty-four books for teens and children. Many of her articles and stories have appeared in the nation's top magazines.

Beverly is a member of The National League of American Pen Women, the Society of Children's Book Writers and Illustrators, and Colorado Christian Communicators. She and her husband, Dave, along with their three teenagers, live in Colorado. She fondly remembers their cockapoo named Cuddles, who used to snore to Mozart!

God give me work
till my life shall end
and life till my work is done.

—Winefred Holtby

I was staring at Penney's display window admiring a blue-striped romper when she came walking toward me.

"Hi, Merry!" her perky voice called.

I smothered my initial response. "Not Lissa Vyner," I muttered to myself. Usually I was super polite, but courtesy didn't come easily around Lissa. Not these days. Not since she'd stolen Jon Klein out from under my nose!

She was standing beside me now, gazing at the current summer teen fashions. I caught the light scent of her perfume. "What's up?" she said.

"Oh, nothing much." I peered into the window and wished she'd go away.

"That outfit would look so cool on you," Lissa said, and I turned to see her pointing at the striped romper. "You should try it on."

And you should go jump in a lake, I thought, feeling instantly guilty for having such lousy thoughts about the girl I'd befriended last Thanksgiving.

"You know how you adore striped things," she was saying. "Especially blue and white."

"Maybe you're right." Quickly, without looking back,

I headed into the store hoping she'd leave me alone. But when I got inside, I realized she'd followed me.

In the junior department, I found the rack of short sets and rompers and searched for my size. Lissa flipped through the rack, too, only on the opposite side. In the petites.

Glancing at her, I noticed Lissa had begun to fill out a bit—in all the right places. Her cheeks had a rosy glow to them, and her blue eyes sparkled when she smiled. In many ways, Lissa looked healthier and happier than ever.

I sighed, thinking about the part I'd played in helping to eliminate her abusive home situation. Her father was still attending group therapy for his drinking problem, but the abuse had stopped. Thank goodness.

Lissa caught me staring at her. I glanced away, avoiding her gaze. *No wonder Jon likes her,* I thought. *She's tiny . . . and pretty. Prettier than most girls I know.*

"Merry?" She circled the clothes rack to stand beside me. "I really get the feeling something's wrong between us," she said softly, almost sadly.

I knew it would complicate things to let her know about my past friendship with Jon. And about our secret word game. "Everything's fine," I said, forcing a smile.

"You say that, Mer, but it seems to me you've been upset for a long time—since before school let out last month." She paused, fingering the price tag on one of the outfits.

"Don't worry, Liss." I held up the blue-striped romper. "I think you're right, this *is* definitely me." And I flounced off to the dressing rooms to try it on.

When I went to pay for the outfit, Lissa was gone. Part

of me was relieved. Even though Lissa and I were friends, she'd become a force to be reckoned with. And I was partly to blame for the conflict between us.

I'd stuck my neck out to help her escape her father's abuse, and invited her to our church youth group. To make her feel more connected to the group, I'd introduced her to my friends—Jon Klein included. Losing *him* was my reward for being a good friend!

I waited in the cashier line while shoppers snatched up bargains around me. Typical for a Fourth-of-July weekend madness sale. To make matters worse, only one register was working. The other wore a handwritten sign that read *Out of order.*

I stared at the sign and thought back to last night and the way my mom had laid into me at supper. *She* was out of order mentioning Levi Zook the way she had. Weeks ago, the next-to-oldest son of our Amish neighbors had asked me out, and against all my friends' wishes—at church and at school—I had accepted. No one seemed to understand why I'd want to hang out with an Amish boy. But they'd never met Levi. Not only was he drop-dead cute, he was responsible and solid. And a true gentleman.

But Mom didn't seem to care about any of that. "Honestly, Merry," she'd said, "you talk about the Amish as though they're somehow better. Dressing plainly and driving buggies doesn't make people closer to God." There was a twinge of resentment in her voice.

I frowned, thinking back to the stressful kitchen scene. Dad kept stirring his coffee—I knew by his movements that he was upset about the conflict, but he didn't interfere. He also didn't join Mom in commenting about me not using my head. That was Dad. Always cool and mostly collected when it came to his daughter. Not that he was partial to me, but I had a feeling that Dad was thinking ahead to next fall when I'd be the only kid left in the house. Skip, my older brother, was headed for college. And Faithie, my twin, had died of leukemia when she was seven.

I wanted to spout off—to tell Mom that just because she didn't understand my Amish friends didn't mean she should talk about them that way. After all, they were peace-loving, simple people—hardworking, obedient people. So what if they wanted to do without fancy clothes, cars, and electricity. Personally, I admired their lifestyle.

But I kept my mouth shut and stirred my iced tea. Like my dad, I believed that a soft answer—or none at all—dispelled anger. Especially in this case. It was plain to see that Mom was wired up, so there was no dealing with anything. Not now.

The more I thought about Mom's remarks, the more it seemed right for her to apologize. She was being totally unreasonable about Levi—thought I was spending too much time with a backward Amish farm boy, as she put it. Thought his philosophy of life was beginning to rub off on me.

What it added up to was this: my personal choices didn't count. And worse, she'd implied that my judgment couldn't be trusted.

The woman's voice at the cash register brought me out of my daze, and I stepped up to the counter to pay for my new clothes. That's when I realized I was starving.

Stress always made me hungry.

After I put away my change, I made a beeline to the nearest fast-food place. It wasn't far—just down the escalator to the first floor and around the corner. But there was such a crowd of shoppers that it took me longer than usual, and by the time I arrived, another long line awaited me.

Undaunted, I slipped into the back of the line behind some tall guy. Standing on tiptoes, I tried to see around him to read the menu. But my shopping bag must've bumped him, because suddenly I found myself staring up—into the face of Jon Klein!

TWO

"Mistress Merry," Jon said, smiling. "What a nice surprise."

I met his gaze with enthusiasm. "Imagine meeting you here."

"Well, what's with . . ." He paused, probably trying to think of another word starting with *w*.

"What's wrong?" I smiled. It had been ages since the Alliteration Wizard and I had played our word game.

His brown eyes sparkled. "Guess I'm a little rusty."

I wanted to shout "Hallelujah," but succeeded in controlling myself. So . . . he *hadn't* introduced Lissa to our special game. This was truly amazing!

"It's been a while for me, too," I said, referring to being out of practice. Now he would know I'd been loyal. Hadn't played the Alliteration Game with anyone. Not Levi Zook, not anyone.

Jon caught the message. I could see the recognition in his eyes.

"I hope you're going on the river hike next weekend," he said.

"I can't. My aunt and uncle are coming. They're

bringing their newborn twins."

"Twins? Really?" He seemed surprised, and then I realized how very long it had been since we'd talked. I realized something else, too. Lissa had not been conveying anything about me to Jon.

Quickly, I filled him in on my life, leaving out certain private things such as the chunks of time I was spending with my Amish neighbors. Especially Levi and his sister Rachel.

"So how long will your relatives be in Lancaster?" he asked as the line moved.

"Just next weekend, I think."

"We should get together and practice our word game sometime." His smile sent my heart sailing, and I waited for him to say that he and Lissa had called it quits. But he didn't.

The girl behind the counter said, "May I take your order, please?"

Jon stared up at the menu board. "I'll have your Number Three Super Special and a large lemonade." Then he turned to me and asked, "Can I buy you lunch?"

"No, but thanks anyway," I said. It was probably a very wise choice on my part, because just then Lissa came breezing past the line.

"Hi again," she said, spotting me.

"Oh, hi," I managed to say.

Jon turned around, obviously happy to see her. "What're you hungry for, Liss?"

"How 'bout a Number Three Super Special and a large lemonade."

I stifled a sigh. Maybe they had more in common than I thought.

Jon was still smiling, only now at me. "Sure you won't join us for lunch?"

"No, really," I replied, my heart sinking fast. "I have tons more shopping to do. I'll eat as I go."

Jon nodded. "Say that with all *g*'s."

Lissa frowned. "What's that mean—say it with all *g*'s?" She looked first at me, then at Jon.

I excused myself and got out of there fast. Worried, I could only imagine the explanation Jon must've conjured up to cover his tracks. As far as I knew, Lissa had no knowledge of the Alliteration Game.

Almost instantly, I changed my mind about shopping. And eating. I hurried to the nearest pay phone, stomach still growling, and called home.

"But, Merry," Mom argued, "it's only been a little over an hour since I dropped you off. I thought you wanted to—"

"Please come get me." I had to avoid running into Jon and Lissa again.

"Is everything okay?" she asked.

"I'm fine." I wished she wouldn't interrogate me like this. "Just come, okay?"

"I'll drop everything." She sounded upset, as if I'd ruined her plans. "I'll meet you at the bus stop in front of Penney's, but it'll take me about twenty minutes."

"I know, Mom." She didn't have to remind me that we lived miles from civilization. On SummerHill Lane— a dirt road smack-dab in the middle of Pennsylvania Amish country.

Hanging up the phone, I glanced outside. I had time to grab a bite. But where? All the fast-food places were *inside* the mall.

I left through the heavy glass doors and took off walking, enjoying the hot July air. It was the clearest, brightest day of the summer so far. A great day to be outdoors. I thought of Lissa and Jon cooped up inside the mall having lunch. And I thought of Levi, probably working outside in his potato field. He would've already eaten lunch—a man-sized dinner, with fried ham, mashed potatoes and gravy, and a fat slice of his mother's strawberry pie.

Levi . . .

What fun the past month had been. Far different from any June in my entire life, but fun. Levi had actually shown me how to cultivate, letting me hold the reins for two mules at once. And there'd been evening hours spent swinging on the rope in the hayloft while Rachel practiced her horse whinny until she and I fell back into the hay, giggling. Levi didn't seem impressed with those moments of hilarity, but he put up with it. And why not? I was his girlfriend, after all.

Levi and I were rarely ever alone, which was just as well, since I was worried his parents might think I was a bad influence.

One night Levi had hitched Apple, the family's beautiful Belgian horse, to their hay wagon. Levi's ten-year-old brother, Aaron, stayed up front with him, chewing on pieces of straw while I sat back in the hay with all four of his sisters. Rachel, almost fifteen, whispered secrets to me about one of the Yoder boys down SummerHill. Nancy, twelve, and Ella Mae, just turned nine, taught me how to sing *Amazing Grace* in German. And six-year-old Susie, the youngest Zook, showed me how to catch fireflies without smashing them.

We were like one big happy family. Distant cousins, really, because my great-great-grandfather also had been a Zook.

I pressed the red pedestrian button at the busy intersection and waited for the light to change. Across the street and halfway down the block, I could see an Amish road stand. There'd be carrots, strawberries, ripe melons, and much more. My mouth didn't exactly water at the prospect of raw vegetables, but a handful of red-ripe strawberries might stop the grumbling in my stomach.

One by one, tourists drove by slowly, most of them gawking. Some had cameras poking out of their car windows. Others milled around, chatting with the girls running the stand.

When I arrived, I noticed a group of people hovering over a child lying in the grass behind the stand. I hurried to investigate.

That's when I spotted Rachel Zook. She was holding something up to the little girl's forehead. I moved in closer, trying to see over the group wearing white prayer caps and long, black aprons atop even longer dresses. Then I caught a glimpse of the petite girl. Susie Zook!

I rushed to Rachel's side. "What happened?"

Rachel looked surprised to see me. "Hello, Merry." She didn't answer my question, and there was a noticeable edge to her voice. Was she upset at me?

I brushed the thought aside. "Did Susie fall?" I persisted, kneeling beside Rachel's sister.

Rachel threw up her hands. "*Ach, Der Herr sie ge-dankt*—thank the Lord she wasn't killed! Susie was climbing that tree"—she pointed to a huge elm—"and, ach, if she didn't up and fall out!"

"Knocked me silly," Susie said, her voice trembling as she sat up.

Rachel nodded. "And now she's all *stroovlich*."

I could see what she meant. Susie's blond braids had come loose, and her long, rose-colored dress was ripped at the seam.

"Poor thing," I whispered. "Can I help?"

Sad-faced, Susie removed the ice to show me her bump. "It's a goose egg, *jah?*" she said.

It was big all right. "Does it hurt?" I asked.

She nodded, tears welling up.

I leaned closer, inspecting her latest battle scar. "Better put the ice back on," I said to Rachel.

Susie reached her hand up to me. "*Ich will mit dir Hehm geh*," she said.

I held her hand in both of mine. "What's she saying?"

Rachel looked worried but avoided my eyes at first. "She wants to go home with you."

The Amish girl to my left leaned over and whispered, "I think she's conked out of her head."

A concussion? I hoped not.

Then I remembered my mom was on her way to meet me. Might even be waiting in front of Penney's by now. "I could take Susie home," I offered, "if there was some way to get her over to the mall." I explained to Rachel that my mother was coming for me.

Rachel eyed the horse and buggy parked off the street.

"Too bad you can't take Apple."

I shook my head. "I'm not taking your horse and buggy through that traffic." Truth was, I'd never taken a horse and buggy anywhere. Sure, I'd ridden in one, but that was much different from actually driving one.

"I can take her," said a familiar voice.

I turned around and there was Levi—eager to help, as always. Rachel explained about Susie's fall and that she should be taken home, out of the heat. "It'll be much quicker if she goes with Merry's mother," Rachel said.

"Jah, good idea." Levi leaned down and gathered his little sister into his arms. With long, careful strides he carried her to the family buggy and gently laid her in the backseat.

Rachel and I followed close behind without talking. The silence between us was deafening.

I spotted the Zooks' market wagon piled up with fresh produce Levi had brought to replenish the road stand. It struck me as curious that Old Order Amish were allowed to ride in a car but couldn't own or drive one themselves.

"Come along, Merry," Levi said, putting on his wide-brimmed straw hat. "You can show me where to meet your mother." He glanced at the market wagon and at Rachel, who promptly left without saying goodbye, scurrying back to help at the road stand. Levi called to her, "I'll come and unload the market wagon after a bit."

She nodded to him, avoiding my wave. It bugged me, this obvious problem between us. But what? What was wrong with Rachel?

THREE

I got into the buggy on the street side, then scooted across to the left side, where Amish women always sat. Levi got in, picked up the reins, and deftly drove Susie and me through the heavy weekend traffic. It seemed strange riding on a modern highway in the Zook carriage. We were somewhat enclosed inside the gray, boxlike buggy, and it helped take away some of the uneasy feeling. But not my hunger pangs.

After one long red light, we arrived safely at the main entrance to the mall. And there we sat in front of Penney's, waiting for my mom to show up.

I tried desperately not to think about Mom's initial reaction to my being here in the Zooks' buggy. Knowing her, she'd be freaking out about it all the way home. In silence, though. Little Susie's presence would keep the conversation at a low ebb . . . until we got home.

Levi turned to glance at Susie resting in the backseat. "How are ya doin' there, little sister?"

She groaned a little. "I'll be better when I get to Merry's house."

He glanced at me. "Why's she wanna go home with you?"

I whispered, "I think the fall might've made her a little confused."

"Oh," Levi said, nodding. "Susie's real spunky—she's always getting herself into scrapes."

I remembered hearing about several of those incidents. "What else?"

Levi let the reins drop over his knees. "Well, once she fell off the hay wagon, and we nearly ran her over."

A tiny giggle escaped from the backseat. I turned around. "Did *you* do that, Susie?"

Her eyes looked brighter now. "Tell about the time when that *alte Kuh* kicked over the milk bucket and stepped on my foot," she said.

"That wasn't funny, Susie," he said. "Ol' Bossy nearly broke your toe!"

Susie discarded the ice bag, letting it drop onto the floor of the buggy. "My head's near froze," she said.

The bump was still protruding. "Better keep the ice handy," I suggested, feeling a bit motherly toward her. "When your head cools off, you should put the ice back on. It'll make the swelling go down."

She nodded, then sat up slowly. "I still wanna go to your house."

"What's so special about my house?" I asked.

"I wanna see your twin. Faithie—the little girl you told me about."

"Oh, you want to see *pictures* of Faithie?"

She smiled, pushing back long, loose strands of hair

away from her face. "Jah." I spied a deep dimple in her left cheek.

I studied Levi then. "Will your mother mind if she comes?"

He shook his head. "I'll head on home and tell her after I unload the market wagon. It'll be about an hour and a half."

Mom pulled into the parking lot just then. Susie waved to her from the back of the buggy. Just as I predicted, Mom looked startled. Quickly, she composed herself and turned the car into the first available spot.

She was getting out of the car when I noticed Jon Klein—with Lissa—coming out of the mall entrance. They were headed right for us!

I grabbed my shopping bag and hopped out of the buggy. Quickly, I turned my back to them. Maybe, just maybe, they wouldn't see me.

Levi reached into the backseat, lifting Susie out of the buggy. Her bare feet dangled out from under her long dress. She was holding the ice bag on her head again.

That's when Mom came over.

Please, Lord, don't let her say anything, I prayed silently. And before she could speak, Levi started explaining things.

"Wouldja mind taking Susie home?" he asked. "She needs to lie down . . . get out of this heat."

"Certainly," Mom said, reaching for the little girl's hand. "Come along, honey." No one had to explain that travel by horse and buggy took much longer than by car. Besides, anyone could see by the size of Susie's bump that she would feel better at home.

I stayed for a moment to thank Levi. That's when I realized Jon and Lissa were standing on the opposite side of the buggy and witnessing the exchange between us.

"Merry?" Lissa said, looking completely aghast. "What's going on?"

Jon looked equally surprised but wasn't asking questions. Not now, at least. He had been quite verbal in the past, asking lots of questions about my interest in the Amish—even wondering why I wanted to spend so much time at the Zooks'. But that had been before school ever let out for the summer.

I had no choice but to entertain a round of introductions. So while Mom was getting Susie settled in the car, I introduced the Alliteration Wizard to the Amish farm boy. The moment would probably go down in history as the most awkward one of my life.

Both boys handled themselves well—Jon reaching out politely for Levi's hand, and Levi accepting the handshake with genuine courtesy. It was Lissa who seemed the most bothered by the encounter. I knew by the way her eyebrows knit together, she was completely bewildered.

Glancing over at our car, I wished now that Mom had come back to make small talk. But she seemed to be waiting for me patiently in the driver's seat. "Guess Mom's ready to go," I said, noting Lissa's eyes growing wide as she surveyed the Amish buggy. I didn't know why she was making such a big deal about this. After all, she'd seen Amish buggies before. Lots of times.

"I'll see ya soon, Merry," said Levi, wearing an enormous grin. "After supper, maybe?"

"Okay," was all I said.

It was next to impossible to ignore the curious look on Jon's face as he began to piece the puzzle together. It was all I could do to keep from blurting out, "Say it with all *p*'s!" before I turned to go.

FOUR

On the drive home, I showed Mom the outfit I'd purchased.

"Cute," she said. And that was the end of that.

I could see she wasn't in the mood for discussion. Evidently, I'd interrupted something important at home by calling her back too soon to get me. Or maybe she was upset at seeing me with Levi in his family buggy. *That* was probably the reason.

I tried not to make too much of it and thought instead of the moment when Jon extended his hand to Levi. It seemed so bizarre for the two of them to meet like that. And with Lissa observing the whole situation!

Thank goodness Mom didn't pound me with questions about it. That is, not until Susie asked, "Didja know my brother is gonna get hitched up with ya, Merry?"

I wanted to melt into the dashboard.

"Then you won't just be my far-off cousin, you'll be my sister, too," she explained from the backseat.

That's when Mom cut loose with questions. Not in a direct sort of way. She did it quite creatively, asking me leading questions in such a way as not to clue in little

Miss Susie with the bump on her head. And the big mouth!

We made a pit stop at the nearest Burger King because by now I was famished. Susie insisted she wasn't hungry, and Mom decided it was wise for her to wait. "A bad fall like that can knock the appetite right out of you," she said, straight-faced.

I laughed a little. "Sounds like some wise old saying."

She didn't seem to find the humor in my remark. Then I knew I was *really* in for it—sooner or later. . . .

When we arrived home, I steadied Susie as we climbed the long staircase to my bedroom. She seemed to be feeling better, and when I checked her forehead, the bump looked smaller.

Mom disappeared to her sewing room without saying much. Eventually, the dam would break, and she'd spill out her concerns about Levi. Again.

In my room, I made Susie relax on my bed. "How do you feel now?" I asked, anxious to know why she'd said that about Levi getting "hitched up" with me.

She grinned that adorable smile, creating a dimple . . . reminding me of Faithie. "I'm better, *Denki*."

"Well, that's good, because I was really worried about you." I sat beside her on the edge of my bed, touching her long, blond hair. Most of it had fallen out of the braids. I got up to find a brush, wondering how on earth to bring her back to the subject of her brother's comment.

Susie didn't seem too interested in having her hair put back in its usual little-girl Amish style. "Can I see the pictures now?" she asked.

"What if I fix your hair while you look at my scrapbook?"

She nodded enthusiastically. "Jah!"

I tossed a hairbrush onto the bed and went to my walk-in closet to locate the powder blue, silver-lined scrapbook—the one that recorded the first seven years of my life with Faithie.

"This is my all-time favorite scrapbook," I said, handing it to her carefully.

She scooted up against the bed pillows and peered at the first page. "Ach, you two are so little here." She stared at the first baby portrait. "Faithie looks smaller than you," she said, her blue eyes filled with curiosity.

I nodded, continuing to braid Susie's near waist-length hair. "Faithie was always small-boned. Everyone said she was tiny for her age. I never thought of her that way, though. Not until after she died."

Slowly, Susie turned to the next page, making endearing comments about the baby twins—my sister and me—as she tiptoed, page by page, through Faithie's short life.

I finished winding her braids around her head long before she finished with the scrapbook. Silently, I sat there, trying to forget what she'd said about Levi and me, letting her take her time gazing into my past.

Suddenly, she leaned forward. "Look, Merry, I see a dimple. Faithie had a dimple just like mine!" She smiled, searching with her pointer finger for the indentation on her own face. "Faithie and I match."

"You're right," I said, realizing there were other similarities between them. Faithie had always been delicate like Susie. And she had fit the role and temperament of the baby of the family even though she was really the *older* twin—by about twenty minutes.

There was something else, too. Faithie had always looked up to me. The way Susie seemed to today.

She closed the scrapbook. "I loved seeing this, Merry," she said softly. "We Amish don't make pictures of ourselves, ya know. But aren'tcha glad ya have these?" Glints of tears sparkled in the corner of her eyes.

"Yes, I'm *very* glad." Lovingly, I held little Susie as she cried soft, sad tears for my sister.

After a long, tender moment, the little girl sat up and wiped her eyes. "Dat and Mam don't ever cry out loud for dead folk," she said.

I understood something about what she was saying. The Amish believed that God allowed people to live just until their work on earth was done. Death was accepted as simply an aspect of life. The patchwork quilt of Amish life consisted of birth, maturity, baptism, marriage, children—lots of them—and death.

"It's just like the crops," Susie remarked, sounding older than her six and a half years. "We plant and water, then the weeding comes, and then the harvest. After that, the dried-up plant goes back into the soil. When someone dies, they get put back in the ground, too."

I knew that Susie's remarks were a result of her Amish training, yet I marveled at her perception of life. I must admit, I didn't agree with it, though. How could I possibly believe that Faithie's work on earth had been finished? She was only seven when she died, for pete's sake!

Carefully, I put my scrapbook away, but now Susie

wanted to look at my pictures on the wall opposite my antique dresser and desk.

"You're looking at what I consider to be my best photography," I said.

She liked the scenery best. That's what she was used to seeing on calendars and wall-hangings at her house. Since the Amish didn't believe in being photographed, only farmscapes and nature were acceptable.

After she had surveyed each one of my framed pictures, I offered her something to drink.

"Jah, some milk," she said, and we went downstairs to the kitchen together. My cats—all four of them—were having their afternoon snack. Compliments of Mom, who'd made herself quite scarce.

"Do ya like Bible names?" Susie asked, watching the cats lap up the cream from the Zooks' dairy.

I wondered if she was thinking about Shadrach, Meshach, and Abednego—three of my cats. "You mean my three Hebrew felines?"

She giggled. "Ach, such funny names for cats, don'tcha think?"

I nodded, opening the strawberry-shaped cookie jar. "Want a cookie?"

"Denki," she said politely.

I took a handful of Mom's chocolate chip cookies out of the cookie jar, placed them on a small plate, and carried it to the kitchen table.

"Do you feel well enough to walk home?" I asked while pouring milk for her. "I can walk over with you if you like."

She looked up at me with her milky white mustache.

"Oh, will ya?" she pleaded as though it meant the world to her. "And can we take the shortcut—through the willows?"

I chuckled. "Okay."

"Then will ya come tonight after supper?" Her cheery, round dollface burst into a wide grin. Leaning close, she whispered, "We can catch lightning bugs."

"Only if you feel up to it," I said, inspecting her forehead. "How's your bump now?"

"Much better." She blinked her saucer eyes.

I felt surprisingly warm and comfortable playing this big-sisterly role to Susie Zook, the youngest of our Amish neighbors. And a very distant cousin.

❧   ❧

After supper, I started cleaning up the kitchen, coaxing my brother to help. Having Skip around was a surefire safeguard. For one thing, I was pretty sure Mom wouldn't launch off on something about Levi and me with Skip hanging around. Besides, even if she did, Skip would probably turn the conversation away from Levi to someone else. Like maybe *his* latest romantic interest, none other than Jon Klein's older sister, Nikki.

Since Dad was working late at the hospital, I couldn't count on him as my ally. It was interesting the way Dad viewed this thing with Levi and me. I remembered the first time I'd asked Mom and Dad about going out with Levi Zook. A really weird, blank expression landed on Dad's face, and I thought for sure all hope was gone. Mom, too. Only *her* facial statement remained the same. Later, after Dad discussed the subject in such a lighthearted, casual manner, Mom started to come around. Just a little. I can't actually say she'd given me the green light, but after I assured her I had no plans to turn Amish, she seemed to relax.

It was true about me not turning Amish. Even though I'd toyed with the idea, spending days on end over at the Zooks' place and "trying on" their beliefs and customs, I really had no idea how being plain could possibly fit into *my* life. Especially now, during the beastly hot, dog days of July. Those heavy, long Amish dresses and aprons would wipe me out!

Give me good old shorts and T-shirts and striped rompers, I thought as I rinsed the plates and silverware, and Skip loaded the dishwasher.

"Hey, Mer, I heard your friend Levi's got big plans for you," he blurted out. Right in front of Mom!

This is truly horrible, I thought, glaring at him. I'd totally overestimated his worth.

"You're joking, right?"

"Guess again." Skip leaned over to stuff a handful of utensils into one of the square-shaped compartments. "The word's out all over SummerHill."

"What are you talking about?"

"I think you already know." He glanced knowingly at Mom.

"Get a grip," I snapped. "Don't you know Levi's been teasing me about marrying him ever since I pulled him half-dead out of the pond?"

Skip nodded. "Say what you want, little girl, but Levi Zook's no fool. He thinks you're gonna marry him when you grow up."

Mom inched closer. "Which means he's probably trying to convert you."

"Really?" I said sarcastically. "Isn't that funny—*I* never noticed any of this."

"Love is blind," Mom stated.

"And the neighbors ain't!" Skip teased.

I turned off the faucet. "Who said anything about love? Levi and I are just . . . just friends." I refused to cry in front of my interrogators.

Skip harrumphed. "That's what everyone says."

"So . . . is that what you and Nikki Klein are, too? Just friends?" It was a low blow, but Skip had it coming.

He snickered. "Wouldn't *you* like to know?"

"Save your breath." And with that, I tromped out of the kitchen.

FIVE

I was thrilled to have an excuse to leave the house. Anything to get away from Skip's weird comments . . . and Mom's insinuations.

Little Susie waited barefoot on the front porch step as I came down the Zooks' long, dirt lane. Her grandfather was relaxing in one of the old hickory rockers and smoking his pipe. His untrimmed beard was long and white, and chubby bare feet stuck out of his black trousers.

"Hullo-o, Merry!" called Susie, getting up and running across the well-manicured lawn. "Come look what Mam gave us to catch the lightning bugs in." She reached for my hand, and we headed back toward the old farmhouse.

I hurried to keep up with her, and when she settled down on the porch step, I noticed only a slight reddish spot where the goose egg had been on her forehead earlier.

Grandfather Zook smiled and nodded as I sat on the porch step. "*Wilkom.* How's our girl?" The way he said it made me wonder if he was in on Levi's plan to convert me. If there even was such a thing.

"Fine, thanks," I said. "And how are you?"

"Oh, fair to middlin'." He took his pipe out for a moment. "It's a fine summer's eve—a fine night for fireflies." He glanced at Susie, who picked up a small canning jar with blades of grass inside.

She peeked at the holes poked through the top. "These are so the lightning bugs can breathe," she explained in her husky little-girl voice. She handed a glass jar to me. "Are ya ready?"

"Wait now," Grandfather Zook said, as though he were expecting dusk to descend on us any minute. "They'll be comin' out by the thousands in just a bit."

And he was right. A few minutes later, hundreds of fireflies began twinkling their bright, intermittent lights, sending their courting signals all the way across the field and up and down SummerHill Lane.

"Let's go!" Susie said.

"Be careful now," Grandfather said. "Don't smash 'um." We knew he was teasing.

Susie's eyes grew wide. "My brother Aaron catches 'um and pulls their tails off."

"Must be a guy thing," I said, remembering that my own father had admitted to pulling their tails off when he was a boy. He'd also stuck the tails on his fingers to make it look as if he were wearing glowing rings.

"But *we* hafta be careful not to hurt 'um," she said.

She was so precocious—carefully reminding me how to capture these twinkly bugs without smashing them. To her, it was a very important aspect of the catching and collecting process—not to kill her exquisite fireflies.

We spent a half hour chasing and catching, turning

our canning jars into miniature lanterns. Off and on the fireflies blinked their luminescent lights, like twinkling stars.

"Look!" Susie cried, staring down at the ground. "We've got 'nough bugs to light up the path."

"Hey, I have an idea. Let's experiment with our lanterns in the willow grove. It's darker there."

"Jah!" she squealed with delight.

Off we ran through the side yard, climbing over the white picket fence. Then, carefully dodging fresh cow pies, we rushed into the pasture. Levi and Aaron waved to us as they unhitched the mules out back, taking them to the barn to feed and water and to rest from the long, hot day. Nancy and Ella Mae ran toward the house barefoot, carrying buckets of vegetables from Rachel's "charity garden."

Carrying our firefly lanterns, Susie and I kept running toward the willow grove. At last, we came to the densest, darkest spot, where the willow branches created a most secret place. A woodland alcove away from the world.

"O-o-oh, this is fun!" Susie held her jar down close to the grassy area beneath her bare feet. The soft, pulsating lights made the willow-sheltered haven seem mysterious as we stood there in the dusk.

"See how much brighter our jars look here," I said. "The darker the night, the brighter the candle."

Susie looked up at me. "Where did ya hear of that?"

I laughed. "Oh, it's just something I read in English class last year."

"It's like the beginning of a poem." She brought the

jar of fireflies up next to her face. "You should hear Grossdawdy's poem."

"Your grandfather writes poetry?"

She nodded. "He's workin' on it every night after supper—till his poem is all done."

This was a surprise. I'd heard that some Amish thought that displays of individuality led to high-mindedness and pride. As far as I was concerned, Grandfather Zook didn't have a prideful bone in his seventy-year-old body.

"Do you like your grandfather's poem?" I asked.

She raised the jar of twinkling fireflies high over her head. "Jah, it's beautiful." Her eyes were full of wonder and excitement. "It's called 'Night of the Fireflies,' " she said in a hushed voice.

"That has a poetic ring to it," I whispered. "Sounds like a truly good poem title."

"Or maybe a book, jah?" she said. "Do ya think you'd ever wanna write one?"

"Write a book?" I had never thought of such a thing.

"I like books. Lots of them." Susie looked around as though her words were secrets. "Levi does, too. Only Mam and Dat don't know."

"What do you mean, they don't know?"

"Promise not to tell?" she said. I had no idea what she was talking about.

I sat down in the soft, wild grass. "Why can't we tell?"

"Levi, he's miserable," she confided, sitting down beside me. "Growing up Amish is real hard for him. Alls he's got to read is the Bible and the *Sugarcreek Budget*."

The latter was a weekly newspaper published in Ohio for Amish all across America.

"What do you think he'd like to read instead?"

"Something else besides what's in the house. Maybe magazines." Susie paused, thinking. "And maybe some books from a Bible college somewheres."

This was the first I'd heard anything about Levi's interest in higher education. Or Bible school. Eight grades of school were all the Amish felt necessary—higher education was useless. Even discouraged.

Susie stared at her bug lantern. "Rachel's mad at him for it."

I wasn't surprised. "I just hope she doesn't think I'm to blame."

Susie shook her head. "It's not yer fault, Merry." She sighed. "Levi's always been *anner Satt Leit*."

I knew she meant her brother was more English, or modern, than Amish. But I wasn't convinced. "Well, he sure looks plain to me . . . except for his new haircut."

She frowned. "Oh, that."

"Does it bother you—Levi's haircut?"

She shrugged her shoulders. "I think he wants ta go English."

I gasped. "Who told you that?"

"Levi did! He said not to tell Mam and Dat . . . and 'pecially not Grossdawdy and Grossmutter."

"Does Rachel know?"

"She's madder'n a hornet 'bout it," she said. "And about you."

So *that's* what was bothering Rachel today in town. It hurt me that she thought I was putting Levi up to such

41

things. "Does Rachel think I'm causing trouble?"

"Jah . . . I think so. She doesn't want Levi to go off and get hitched up with you, like he's always saying."

I was shocked. "He actually talks like that?"

She nodded. "All the time."

"In front of your parents, too?"

"Levi's a *Deihenger*—a little scoundrel."

"He's not so little, really," I said. "He's nearly seventeen now." Levi's birthday was coming up at the end of the summer. In August.

"Grossdawdy wanted him to get baptized this summer, but he won't. He's bein' stubborn."

It seemed a little unsettling hearing this news about Levi—and Rachel—from their little sister. But Susie had a daring streak in her, and I couldn't be sure, but it wouldn't surprise me if someday she started talking about leaving the Amish, too.

I remembered what Mom and Skip had said about Levi making plans to convert me. Were they ever wrong!

Susie started counting her fireflies, first in English, then in German. And when she finished, she began to hum a familiar tune—*What a Friend We Have in Jesus*.

I joined in, trying to remember the German words. When I forgot, Susie helped me on the second verse.

It was truly enchanting here, singing softly like this in the middle of the willow trees. Spending time with a little girl so much like Faithie—my long-ago twin. I leaned back in the grass listening to the sounds around us as we sang our song. It seemed as though all of nature wanted to join in on the last stanza, and one by one, tiny creatures of the night began to emerge from their hollows.

"Listen! I hear something," Susie whispered.

I stopped singing. "What?"

She put her jar down and kneeled up, cupping her hand around her ear. "Ach, there it is again!"

I peered into the darkness on all sides of us. I really didn't think there was anything to be afraid of, but I wanted Susie to know I could take care of her . . . in case there was.

"We're safe here, jah?" she asked.

"Don't worry." I glanced around the familiar area. I'd grown up playing in this thick strip of trees. The willows grew in long rows, dividing our property from the far edge of the Zooks' pasture to the west of their farmhouse. I knew every inch of this grove.

Rachel and I had spent many hours here. Faithie, too. It was a truly splendid place to conduct secret meetings, make mystery-solving plans, and . . .

Susie jumped. "Didja hear that?"

"I hear it now."

She clung to her glass jar.

A sound, almost like a horse whinny but not quite, rippled through the stillness. It sounded close. Maybe a few yards away.

"Let's get out of here!" I grabbed her hand and we ran through the trees, pushing tendrils of long, weeping willow branches away from our faces. At last, we reached the open pasture and the circle of light coming from the outside yard light behind the house.

"Are we safe now?" Susie asked.

"Looks like it to me," I said, noticing her fireflies were gone. "Oh no, did you drop your jar?"

She looked down. "Ach, where could it be?"

"Stay here. I'll go search for it."

"No, Merry! Don't go back."

I knelt down, looking into her angel face. "Don't worry, I'll find it. Here, hold my jar—keep it safe, okay?"

She nodded, her lower lip protruding. "I'll stand right here till ya come."

I hurried back toward the willows and was out of breath by the time I found the spot where Susie and I had sat in the grass.

It was dark now, no moon to speak of. *The jar of fireflies should be easy to spot*, I thought as I searched the area.

That's when I heard the strange sound again. My ears tingled. The sound was definitely a horse, but a horse in desperate need.

I envisioned a colt caught in the thicket. Should I call for Levi's help?

Walking in the direction of the neighing, I felt truly courageous—at first. Then, as it started up again, I heard rustling behind the thick, wide trunk of a willow tree.

My throat turned to cotton. Even if I had wanted to call for help, I—

Suddenly, whatever was behind the tree began to thrash around. I was close enough to touch it!

My heart pounded in my throat.

Legs cramped, I inched backward, unsure of my next move. The thought crossed my mind that I should run for my life. I paused, trying to think rationally. What could possibly cause so much commotion?

Part of me wanted to forge ahead—find out what was lurking in the darkness. But another part of me—my legs—absolutely refused to move.

SIX

I backed away from the tree and the strange sounds. It was a cowardly act, but I'd promised to rescue Susie's lightning bugs.

In the distance, I spotted a glowing object. Off and on it flickered, a few yards from where Susie and I had whispered our secrets just minutes before.

I made my legs move toward the radiant jar.

"Stop!" a voice rang out.

I froze. "Who's there?"

The scratchy-throated voice of someone pretending to be a horse broke the stillness.

"Rachel? Is that you?"

Slowly, hesitantly, she emerged from behind the tree. Rachel's *kapp*, her white prayer bonnet, had slipped halfway off, and her apron looked mussed. "Ach, I can't fool ya," she said, wrestling with a stray willow branch. She tossed it aside.

"Rachel, what on earth are you doing? You nearly scared the wits out of your little sister—and me." I looked to see if Susie was still standing in the side yard where I'd left her. The blinking fireflies in the jar told me she was.

Rachel's voice sounded edgy. "Guess I oughta be sorry, but . . ." Her voice trailed off.

I knew why she'd scared us. Rachel was mad.

We walked all the way down the slope to Susie's jar of fireflies, then out of the willows and through the pasture in silence.

When Rachel spoke, her voice trembled. "I should be awful ashamed, cousin Merry."

I wanted to say *you're right*, but I didn't. "Look," I snapped, "I'm not putting ideas into Levi's head, if that's what you think."

"Well, I think ya must be."

"Well, I'm not."

"Maybe ya just oughta leave him be," she huffed.

Now *I* was mad! I stopped in front of the picket fence. "In case you didn't know it, Rachel, it wasn't my idea to be Levi's girlfriend, and if you think it was, maybe you'd better go talk to him!"

It was the first time we'd ever exchanged harsh words.

"Let him go steady with an Amish girl," she said. It was a desperate plea.

"If that's what he wants, fine with me," I retorted. But I knew better. Levi liked me better than all the girls in his Amish crowd. He'd said so!

I glanced over my shoulder at the willows. "I know you were listening in on Susie and me before, so don't say you weren't."

"I wouldn't lie to ya." She picked up her long skirt and climbed over the fence.

Of course, she wouldn't lie. After all, Rachel was Amish, through and through.

When we reached Susie near the yard light, I handed over the second jar of fireflies. "You scared me," Susie told Rachel.

"I'm sorry," Rachel said, touching her sister's head. "It was foolish."

I wasn't in the mood to hang around, not the way Rachel had been acting, so I started to tell Susie goodbye.

"Please don't leave yet, Merry," she pleaded. "It's still early. Maybe Grossdawdy will read ya his poem."

Rachel brushed off her apron, then turned and headed for the back door without saying goodbye—so foreign to the way she usually treated me. Susie didn't seem to notice the friction between her big sister and me, though. She reached for my hand, leading me around to the front porch where both Zook grandparents were sitting and chatting in their matching hickory rockers.

The two of them looked sweet relaxing there, and I began to forget about the trick Rachel had pulled in the willows.

"Grossdawdy, how's your poem comin'?" Susie asked, going up the porch steps to lean on his shoulder.

"*Jah, well Ich bins zufreide*," he said softly with a smile. "All right. I'm satisfied."

"Could ya read it for Merry?" she pleaded.

Grandmother Zook shook her head. "He still has a ways to go yet."

"That's okay. I can wait," I said, leaning on the railing. "Susie told me the title—it sounds beautiful."

"Jah," Grandma Zook said, nodding her head up and down as she rocked. "Wonderful-*gut* title."

"Where did you get the idea for it?" I asked.

He stroked his white beard. "From my youngest granddaughter here." He looked up at Susie, grinning. "She loves them fireflies," he said. "And she's a lot like 'um, too. Shining her little light for the world to see."

"*I'm* not a lightning bug!" Susie exclaimed, then burst into a stream of giggles.

"Hush, child," Grandma said. "It's eventide. Time to reflect on the day . . . time to read the Bible some."

"And pray," Grandfather added. "Practice saying 'The Lord's Prayer.' "

Susie bowed her head and folded her hands. " 'Our father which art in heaven,' " she began, reciting the entire prayer.

When we opened our eyes, Grandfather whispered, "Now in German," with a grand twinkle in his eyes. And Susie started over again.

Afterward, the screen door opened and Levi came out. "Time for evening prayers." His face broke into a broad smile when he spotted me.

"I better say good-night," I told Susie.

She came over to me, putting her bare foot between the slats in the white porch railing. "Will ya come tomorrow?"

I smiled at her, warmed by her attention. "If you want me to."

"I do, I do!" she sang.

"Susie!" Grandmother Zook said as she got up off the rocker and headed into the house. "Come along."

Susie picked up the jars of fireflies. "Quick," she whispered. "We hafta let 'um go."

"Better not keep your family waiting," I warned, remembering her grandmother's tone of voice.

Opening the lid on her jar, Susie looked at me, expecting me to do the same. "Ready, set—now!" When I opened mine, a wispy spray of light floated out.

"Truly beautiful," I whispered.

Susie turned to go inside, and I noticed Levi still waiting at the screen door. "Merry," he called to me. "I hafta talk to ya."

I was curious about the urgency in his voice. "Something wrong?"

He shook his head. "Tomorrow night I'll pick you up in my buggy."

"I . . . I don't know if I should," I said, thinking about the things Rachel had said before. "Maybe we should talk about it."

He frowned. "Well, then can ya meet me in the barn after last milking?"

"Okay."

So it was set. I would meet with Levi in the barn, probably the hayloft, so we could discuss getting together later—to talk about something else. This was truly bizarre!

SEVEN

When I arrived home, Dad was enjoying a bowl of chocolate ice cream. His Bible was open on the table. I pulled out a kitchen chair and sat down.

"How was *your* day?" he asked, looking up.

I told him about spending the day with Susie Zook. "She's real spunky, that girl," I said, explaining about her fall from the tree. "Susie's fearless—I don't think she's afraid of anything."

Dad nodded. "Maybe she knows this verse in the Old Testament." He moved the Bible closer to me.

"Which one?" I leaned over the table.

"Here—Second Chronicles, thirty-two, seven. 'Be strong and courageous. Do not be afraid or discouraged.' "

"Maybe you're right." I laughed. "But I never hear Susie quoting Bible verses. Not Rachel either. Some Amish don't teach their children to memorize scriptures."

"But they *do* get their children outside and working, doing chores, and learning new things real young. That toughens them up." He glanced at the ceiling as though he was thinking back. "I remember when Levi was about six. Old Abe had him out plowing the field by himself."

"That young?"

Dad scooped up more ice cream. "Come to think of it, Levi was out driving a pony cart up and down SummerHill Lane around the same age."

No wonder Levi's so comfortable driving a buggy, I thought, remembering how he'd steered Apple through congested traffic today.

"Well, little Susie's just like him," I said. "But catching fireflies is her big interest now." I described how she and I had run around putting them in canning jars.

"I did the same thing as a kid. We'd catch them and pull their tails off. The light would keep shining for a long time afterward."

"That's gross." I glanced around the kitchen, even leaned my chair back and peered into the dark dining room. "Where *is* everyone?"

"Skip's out on a date, and your mother's visiting Miss Spindler. Took a plate of cookies over to her."

"Old Hawk Eyes," I said, referring to the neighbor behind us on Strawberry Lane. "Usually by this late in the summer, she has the neighborhood news posted on every street corner."

Dad chuckled. "What would it be like, living for the sheer pleasure of gossiping?"

"It's gotta be mighty boring, I mean, it sorta tells you something about *her* life, right?"

"Can you imagine how hot her phone lines must be?" He dug into more ice cream. "Speaking of phones, Lissa Vyner called about thirty minutes ago."

I didn't have to guess why she was calling. She was probably still recuperating from seeing me with Levi today.

Reluctantly, I scooted my chair out from the table. "Mind if I use your phone?"

Glancing up, he mumbled something and nodded. I headed down the hall to Dad's private study and closed the door.

Lissa answered the phone on the first ring.

"Hi," I said. "You called?"

"Merry, have you lost your mind?" I should've known this wasn't going to be friendly.

"That's it, cut right to the chase," I muttered.

"Look, Mer, I know you're mad about something."

"What're you talking about?"

She breathed into the phone. "Well, if you won't level with me, at least maybe you can clear up something else."

Here it comes, I thought.

"I couldn't believe it when I saw you in that . . . that . . ."

"Amish buggy," I stated matter-of-factly. "Repeat after me: B-u-g-g-y."

"Merry! What's wrong with you?"

"Maybe I should ask *you* that question."

"I'm just worried," she said. "What's wrong with that?"

"You're worried because I happen to have some very nice Amish friends?"

"C'mon, you know what I'm talking about," she said.

"Oh, *do* I?"

Lissa sighed into the phone. "You're making this hard."

"Well, I'm sorry," I said, ready to cut this discussion short. "Why don't you just spell it out?"

"Okay. Why are you still hanging out with that Amish kid?"

"And why not?"

She was obviously past the boiling point. "We . . . I . . . thought it was just a crush, that you'd be over Levi Zook by now."

"Well . . . welcome to the real world!"

"What's *that* supposed to mean?" She sounded completely baffled. "You're not actually going out with him, are you?"

"Why should I change my mind now?"

"It's just that I hoped you'd get tired of being with those Amish farmers and . . . and come back—you know, to us."

"Who's us?"

"Your *real* friends."

I almost choked. "Real friends don't do this."

"Merry, you're turning the whole thing around. I called to tell you that I miss you. So does everyone else."

Jon, too? I wondered.

"I got a postcard from Chelsea today," she continued. "She's in California at Disneyland."

"I know . . . so?"

"She asked how you were doing, like she was concerned."

Chelsea Davis and I had known each other since grade school. Recently, we'd gotten better acquainted when we teamed up on a social studies project at the end of the school year.

"Chelsea doesn't have to worry," I said. "And neither do you. I'm having the time of my life. And if you can't understand that, then I guess we have no reason to be talking right now."

"But Merry—"

I hung up. Just like that—hung up the phone.

❧   ❧

The next morning I slept in. Saturdays were made for sleeping late, especially when it was so warm and humid outside. Two more days before the sizzling Fourth.

Halfway between consciousness and drowsiness, while curling up with my pillow, I thought of Lissa. I'd done the wrong thing by hanging up on her, even though I truly felt she had it coming. Doing the right thing wasn't always easy, especially for an impulsive person like me, but the fact that I'd led Lissa to the Lord made me feel irresponsible.

The whole thing had gotten out of hand, starting with the way she'd accused me of losing my mind just because I was friends with Levi. After breakfast, I thought of calling her to apologize, but Dad was involved with some computer work in his study, and I didn't want to risk being overheard on another phone in the house.

Mom was busy baking for the Fourth of July. She had the idea that a holiday—*any* special day—was an automatic excuse to cook up a storm. And company or not, we always had oodles of food around. Even for incidental days like April Fool's Day and Mother-in-Law Day.

I hurried upstairs to my room, hoping I wouldn't be asked to divide egg whites or measure sugar for Mom's pies. The truth was, I felt betrayed. She'd sided last night with my brother on the Levi issue, accepting what Skip had said—that Levi was out to convert me—as fact. After all, I was her daughter, her own flesh and blood. She ought to know me better than that!

I'd tried to block last night's conversation out of my mind, but her words rang in my memory: *Love is blind.*

How could Mom jump to such a conclusion? Why did she have such a hard time remembering what it was like being thirteen, nearly fourteen?

A brief, yet intensely satisfying feeling stirred through me as I reveled in my secret knowledge. Levi had no intention to convert me to Amish. But he *did* have plans . . . for himself. Now if I could just hear them straight from Levi's lips.

I set to work organizing my room, sorting through scenic snapshots I'd taken last month, arranging them according to subject matter: flowers, trees, the banks of the Conestoga River, and an old covered bridge. My plan was to purchase another scrapbook with next week's allowance.

That finished, I played with my cats, forgetting about calling Lissa. Then I really lost track of time while going through my bookcase. Looking through my poetry collection, I found some great stuff to show Susie's grandfather.

After lunch, Mom asked me to take a lemon-meringue pie over to Miss Spindler. I watched as she placed it carefully inside her cloth-lined pie basket.

"What's the occasion?" I asked.

"It's almost the Fourth, you know. Just wanted to do something nice for Ruby Spindler."

I headed out the back door and past the white gazebo in our yard. Old Hawk Eyes was sitting on her patio thumbing through a craft magazine when I arrived.

"Well, hello there, dearie." She got up from her chaise lounge. "How's every little thing?"

"Fine, thanks." I held out the pie. "Mom made this for you."

She peeked inside the basket. "Ah . . . my very favorite." Turning back to me, she said, "Well, now, Miss Merry, you tell that momma of yours a big thank you. Ya hear?"

I nodded. "I will. And you have a nice Fourth of July."

"Well, I certainly hope to," she replied. "And you . . . you will, too, won'tcha, dear?" A curious expression crossed her wrinkled face. "But of course, the Amish don't celebrate *that* holiday, do they?"

Now I was the one with the curious look.

"Honey-girl, don't look so surprised," she went on. "Everyone 'round here knows 'bout you and that Zook boy. Personally, I think it's kinda sweet—if I say so myself."

"Excuse me, Miss Spindler," I said. "What is it everyone knows?"

Her mouth drooped. "Well, I'll be . . ." She paused. "You really don't know what you're getting yourself into, do you, darlin'?"

I could see this had the potential for turning into a long, drawn-out conversation, and I certainly didn't want to feed her gossip column with my personal views and opinions. It was flat out none of her beeswax about Levi and me!

She tilted her head to one side. "Are you all right?"

"Just fine, thanks. Now, if you don't mind, I better go."

My heart pounded heavily as I ran across her backyard and down the slope to ours. I could never be sure, but I was almost positive Miss Spindler was watching my every move. I could feel her eyes boring into me. That's what the old lady was all about. That's why Skip and I, and Rachel and Levi—all of us—called her Old Hawk Eyes.

Knowing how she was, I should've dismissed her outrageous comments for what they were. Outrageous and absolutely false. But for some reason, I let her words sink into me long into the afternoon, on until it was time to meet Levi after milking.

❧　　❧

"Wilkom, Merry," he said as I came into the barn.

"Hi." I spied the long rope in the hayloft. It was the same rope Levi had been swinging on when he asked me to be his girl. The same rope I'd flown on across the haymow, screaming with fright the very first time—as a little girl.

"*Was ist letz?*" he asked. "What is wrong?"

I looked around to see if we were alone. "Is it safe to talk here?"

He took off his straw hat and wiped his forehead. "Dat will be comin' in soon, so best hurry."

I didn't waste any time. "I'm sorry, Levi, but I'm not going anywhere with you in your buggy tonight."

His eyebrows shot up.

"Your family's concerned . . . they don't want me to be your girlfriend."

He put his hat back on. "I hear in your voice that there's more to it, jah?"

I sighed. "Everyone's talking, Levi. People who don't even know you—and others—are saying things."

"Ach, what things?"

I moved closer to him. "That you're thinking of leaving the Amish." I studied him closely, tracing with my eyes every familiar line in his tan face. This fantastically handsome face I'd known since I was a kid. "Is it true?"

"You will be the first to know," he said confidently, as though he'd already made up his mind. He reached for my hand. "There's so much I wanna tell ya."

Gently, I pulled my hand away, and it was a good thing, too, because just then Abe Zook came into the barn the back way, through the cow door.

"We hafta talk more," he said with serious eyes, and I knew by the tone of his voice it couldn't wait.

No matter what, I would meet Levi later tonight. With or without the buggy ride.

EIGHT

At dusk, I took my poetry books over to Grandfather Zook. He was sitting with his wife in the front yard when I came. For more than an hour, they watched Susie and me catch fireflies. This time we filled nearly three-fourths of each little jar. When we returned, we showed our bug-lanterns to Grandfather Zook.

"*Des is gut*," he said, holding the jars in his calloused hands. "God has put His light in these here critters."

"Jah!" Susie said, grinning at me. "Now we hafta let 'um go."

"So soon?" I stared at the twinkling lights in my glass jar. "We just caught them."

"Maybe it's time for me to read ya my poem," Grandfather said. He grunted a bit as he got out of his lawn chair. Grandma Zook followed him up to the porch and waited along with us.

Soon, he was back carrying a pad of yellow-lined paper. "Here we are." And he sat down in his old hickory rocker.

Susie crept in closer and sat at her grandfather's feet. She pulled her knees up under her chin, her long dress and pinafore apron billowing out over her bare feet.

Grandfather peered over the top of his glasses. "Now, when I do this"—and here he pointed to us—"both of you let your fireflies go."

"Okay!" Susie cried, obviously enjoying the dramatic aspect. "We're going to act out Grossdawdy's poem." She giggled a bit.

Her grandfather waited without speaking, and Susie settled down. Then he began to read:

"Night of the Fireflies"
by Jacob Zook

'Tis the night when martins sing,
'Tis the night for crows to caw,
And dusk comes soft on tiptoes,
In time for the firefly ball.
Come one, come all,
To the firefly ball.
Dance with 'um, laugh with 'um,
Run straight and tall.
'Tis the night when fireflies blink,
'Tis the night for stars to fall,
And dusk comes wearing red satin,
To await the firefly ball.
Come one, come all,
To the firefly ball.
Dance with 'um, laugh with 'um,
Run straight and tall.

Grandfather pointed to us and we knew it was the cue to set our fireflies free. We opened our canning jars, releasing a spray of dazzling light as he read the third verse.

'Tis the night of the fireflies,
'Tis the night of grand light,
And dusk wears honeysuckle,
To dance at the firefly ball.
Come one, come all,
To the firefly ball.
Fly with 'um, flit with 'um,
Run straight and tall.

He stopped reading and set his pad down in his lap. "It seems to me there oughta be one more verse." He looked a little dreamy-eyed.

"Wow," I whispered. "I think it's great just the way it is!"

"I told ya," Susie said, jumping up. "Grandfather's a real poet."

I was curious. "How did you learn to write poetry?"

"Oh, every now and again I'll scribble some things down," Grandfather said. "Sometimes the words just seem to fit together." He sighed audibly.

It was getting late, and Levi would soon be coming for me. I hated to disturb the serene moment but said my goodbyes to Susie and her grandfather. "Keep my poetry books as long as you like," I said before leaving.

"Denki," Grandfather said, waving. "Come again, jah?"

"I will," I promised, hurrying down the Zooks' lane to SummerHill. I thought of Susie and the fun we'd had. And Grandfather Zook's lovely poem. Now, what on earth was Levi going to discuss with me?

❧   ❧

An hour later, a light splashed on my bedroom window. When I stuck my head out to investigate, I saw Levi below with a flashlight. "Can ya talk now?" he asked.

"Meet me in the gazebo," I said and hurried downstairs.

Mom and Dad were relaxing, watching TV in the family room when I headed for the kitchen for some matches.

"Where're you off to?" Mom called.

"I'll be in the backyard," I said, taking the matches along to light the citronella candles that kept the mosquitoes away. I didn't say why I was going or who I was going to meet. But Mom was smart about things —she'd probably already figured it out.

I heard Skip snicker. "Be sure and take your dumb cats with you. Maybe they'll scare your boyfriend away."

"Whatever." I closed the screen door behind me. They had no idea what they were saying. Levi was the sweetest, kindest boy I'd ever known.

He sat on the gazebo step, waiting. Shadows from the giant maples surrounding the white latticework played around him. I couldn't see him clearly at first. Then, when I was within a few feet, I caught a clear glimpse. Levi was wearing contemporary clothes!

"What on earth?" I said.

His hair had been cut and styled weeks ago, so that was nothing new, but the blue jeans and button-down short-sleeve shirt . . . well, this new look was completely unsettling. Levi Zook could've passed for any other modern kid around!

"Whaddaya think?" he asked.

I avoided his question. "What does this mean?"

"It only means that I'm trying on English ways."

My throat felt dry. Was this what he meant earlier today? Was this the way I would be the first to know?

"I hope this doesn't have anything to do with me." I didn't want to sound presumptuous.

"Don'tcha worry, Merry. I've been thinkin' about this for as long as I can remember."

"Going English—really?"

"Jah," he said, moving over to make room for me to go into the gazebo and light the bug-repellent candles. "I'm not happy farmin', and I wanna know what's in books. I'm hungry for learnin'. Do ya understand?"

I was relieved about his reasons. "You're following your heart then, right?"

He nodded, looking at me as I motioned for him to sit on a padded lawn chair. "In another way, too." He came and pulled the chair up next to mine, then reached for my hand. I could feel the coolness of his hand against my knuckles. My heart did a little dance.

Yee-ikes! What was he going to say now?

"I know you're real young and all, Merry," he began. "But I've been waitin' a long time to ask you this."

"Wait, Levi—don't say anything! Please!" I had to stall him. I wasn't ready to be proposed to. Not two months away from turning fourteen. Sure, if I were Amish, maybe a boy might ask me to go steady—but this?

"I'm sorry," he said, his voice mellow and sweet. "There's nothin' to worry about. I would never wanna hurt you. You see, I love ya, Merry. Plain and simple. Always have."

He sounded terribly convincing, even without a full moon to enhance the setting. Sincerity and honesty were two of Levi's many good traits. And the way he looked, wearing modern clothes—dressed like my own brother or any other boy in town—made me more inclined to want to believe him.

I started to speak, but his finger touched my lips gently. "You don't have to say it back. We have lots of time ahead of us."

"Time?"

"I want some more book learning. Maybe go to a Bible college somewheres. But I will *not* be a farmer."

"What will your parents say? How long can you live at home?" I worried that he was deciding things too quickly.

"Mam and Dat already know some of this," he explained.

"Rachel, too?"

"Jah, Rachel . . . and the other children."

"You know, Rachel thinks I'm to blame for this. Can't you explain the reasons why you want to leave? It would help things between Rachel and me if you did."

"I can if she'll just believe me."

"Please don't quit trying," I pleaded. "It's important for me to have her as my friend. Little Susie, too."

He smiled, his eyes twinkling in the candlelight. "Susie loves ya, Merry," he said. "She thinks you're her special playmate—her firefly friend."

I remembered the dimple in her left cheek and the similarities between her and my twin, Faithie. "I love her, too."

He leaned back against the lattice frame. "I s'pose she'll wanna read lots more books than Mam and Dat can offer. Just like her big brother."

I told him what she'd already said about wishing there were more books in the house.

"I think maybe little Susie and I are cut from the same cloth." We talked a while longer, then he pulled some keys out of his pocket. "Wanna go for a little spin?"

I gasped. "You have a car?"

"A couple of my cousins and I went together and bought a real nice one."

My heart sank. "Won't this bring more trouble for you?"

He didn't respond to my question, jingling his car keys instead. The sound brought Abednego, my fat, black cat, out from under the gazebo. "Here kitty, kitty," Levi called.

Abednego arched his back, showing instant dislike.

"Don't mind him," I said. "Abednego has an obvious disdain for most all of the human male species."

He chuckled, then changed the subject. "Shouldn't ya ask your parents' permission to ride?"

I knew he'd gotten his driver's license, but I was also familiar with the way he handled a horse and buggy. "I don't call you Zap 'em Zook for nothing," I said, laughing.

He didn't seem to mind the joke. "We won't go too far up SummerHill," he coaxed.

"I better not, Levi." Then I asked, "Are you still running around with that wild bunch of boys?"

"I've sowed my wild oats, Merry. More and more I go

to Bible studies at my Mennonite friends' house."

I knew some of the Amish didn't allow independent study of the Bible. They viewed the bishop as the dispenser of spiritual wisdom and truth. And certain scriptures were used as examples over and over in the preaching services.

"I wanna know more. I . . ." He paused. "I wanna be a preacher, Merry, a minister of the gospel."

Levi, a preacher? I thought. *How truly exciting!*

I wanted to hug Levi, but I only squeezed his hand. "That's wonderful," I said.

"The Bible, it's so plain about showin' the way," he said with shining eyes. "I wanna share the good news with everyone! Everyone I meet!"

I leaped up out of my chair. "Go into all the world and tell the good news. You're following the Lord's command, 'Rev.' Levi Zook!"

He chuckled. "Merry Hanson, you'll make a fine preacher's wife someday."

"That's what you think," I said.

NINE

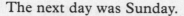

The next day was Sunday.

Lissa and Jon sat together during Sunday school and church as if they were a regular couple. It was becoming less difficult for me to see them together, maybe because they were *always* together. Still, sometimes I missed Jon—and our secret alliteration game.

During the singing, I thought about Levi and the long talk we'd had last night. He seemed determined to follow God's plan for his life.

I remembered the verse in Second Chronicles that Dad had read to me: "Be strong and courageous. Do not be afraid or discouraged."

Now that Levi had a goal in mind, he seemed stronger than ever. I liked unwavering strength in a guy. But . . . I also liked Jon Klein and the way we'd hit it off during our middle-school years together. Why did things have to be so complicated?

After church, Jon and Lissa came up to me in the parking lot. Lissa was all ears—eyes, too—when Jon asked if I was ready for the Alliteration Challenge.

I gulped, trying to hide my delight and surprise. "Are you serious?"

"When's a good time for you?" he asked.

"I'm out of practice," I told him, nearly dying of embarrassment as Lissa's eyes started to bulge. "Maybe we should wait."

"What're you talking about?" Lissa demanded.

He hadn't told her!

"It's, uh . . ." Jon glanced at me, his eyes begging for assistance.

"It's just a thing," I blurted.

Lissa's eyes widened. "A thing? Like *what* thing?"

I had no intention of filling her in on Jon's and my private word game. But it was Jon's problem now—he'd gotten it started. I stared at him, hoping he'd take my lead and say something amazing to appease his girlfriend.

He tried to explain. "You know how some friends have inside jokes?" He sounded terribly patronizing. "Well"—and here he glanced at me with the most endearing look—"Merry and I have an inside game, I guess you could call it."

"Merry and you?" she echoed.

Jon nodded. "It's just something we—Merry and I—do."

I could see this vague explanation wasn't going to suit Lissa. Not at all. She whirled around and stormed across the parking lot, not looking back.

"Uh, maybe that wasn't the best approach," I said, slightly concerned. "She's obviously upset."

The corner of his mouth wrinkled up, and I suspected that he'd set this up on purpose. "Lissa just doesn't understand that people can have more than one good friend at a time," he said.

I noted that he'd almost said *girlfriend!*

"Well, I hope she gets over it," I said.

"Say that with all *e*'s!" he teased.

"Okay, I will." I paused to think, feeling lousy about Lissa leaving like that. Seconds passed, then it came to me. "Eventually, endurance evolves to an end."

Jon wore a quizzical expression. "Huh?"

"I told you I was out of practice!"

"That wasn't so bad, really." He flashed his wonderful smile. "Just didn't make any sense."

"I'm sorry about what happened just now with Lissa."

He shrugged a little as though it wasn't something to worry about. "She gets overpossessive sometimes."

I struggled with mixed emotions. It was exciting being with Jon again—like old times. The passion for words was still strong between us. But Lissa was also my friend, and I'd played a big role in making her very upset.

❧   ❧

After dinner, Lissa called. "Why were you flirting with Jon like that?" She sounded more accusing than interested in a genuine answer.

"Well, I don't know what to tell you," I said, making an attempt at courtesy. "I didn't think I was flirting."

"C'mon, Merry, you were!"

I sighed. "Well, I guess if you say so, then I was."

"So . . . you're admitting it?"

"Isn't that what you want to hear?" Frustration was a way of life with this girl!

She exhaled into the phone. "What I want is for you to stay away from Jon. He's mine, and that's the way it's gonna stay."

"Well, I understand how you feel, Lissa. I'm sorry you misunderstood, really. And I'm sorry about hanging up on you yesterday. Honest." I must've sounded a tad too sweet, even though I meant to be sincere.

Anyway, my words obviously backfired on me—now it was *her* turn to hang up on me. Except Lissa didn't just hang up. She slammed down the phone.

What was going on? Was Lissa really and truly afraid of losing Jon? And if so, why?

TEN

The Sunday evening service was canceled so people could spend time with their families since it was the night before the Fourth.

Dad knew he would probably be busy in the ER tomorrow. More accidents happened on a big holiday than at any other time, he often said. Kids mishandling firecrackers; people drinking and driving. He'd be working all day tomorrow. That's how it was when your dad was the head honcho—the best—on a city hospital trauma team.

Dad was stretched out on his chaise lounge in the shade of the gazebo. He was taking it real easy this afternoon. Two bluebirds and three sparrows sparred over who got dibs on the birdbath in our side yard.

Things were quiet. Peaceful. Skip was out on a date with Nikki Klein, playing badminton at her house. Made me wonder if Lissa and Jon were making it a foursome. I tried not to think about them, though. Lissa's response to my apology was troubling. I wondered how I could patch things up with her.

Mom was taking her usual Sunday afternoon walk.

She liked to walk briskly several times a week. Did it like clockwork—especially on Sundays after dinner. The steep jaunt up Strawberry Lane, the road behind our house, was a workout for anyone. Fit or not.

"It's good for her," Dad said, reaching for his iced tea. "Gets her heart rate up."

"What about you, Dad?" I sipped on a tall glass of lemonade. "Shouldn't you be exercising, too?"

He agreed with me. "Guess I'm getting old and worn out, though. Sometimes it's just easier to take a nap, especially on a hot afternoon."

I poked him playfully. "Oh, Daddy, you're not *that* old."

"The big five-o is coming up fast," he said, looking serious. Too serious.

"Oh, so what. Fifty's just another number." I hoped that would cheer him up. Lately, it seemed every time he mentioned his age, a cautious look crossed his face. It made me feel uneasy.

Later, we talked about Amish doctrine and how it was different from our beliefs. When Dad was close to dozing off, I mentioned Levi's interest in becoming a preacher.

His eyes popped open. "Levi Zook?"

"Yep."

"Well, if that doesn't take the cake!"

"Will it be tough for him—leaving the Amish eventually?"

"Not nearly as hard as if he'd gone along with baptism and then left. This way, he'll always have the fellowship of his family and friends. He won't have to suffer the shunning."

I was relieved. Levi didn't need the stress of abandonment along with everything else. We talked more about Amish life and their tradition. Then, during a lull in the conversation, I glanced at Dad and noticed he'd given in to an afternoon nap.

That's when *I* went for a walk. I decided my heart needed stimulation, too. Even though I was only pushing fourteen!

Many more cars were driving up and down SummerHill today. More than usual. Tons of tourists were in Lancaster County for the Fourth. And by the looks of the traffic, lots of them had discovered the best views of Amish farmland were out here off the beaten tracks.

Halfway down the road, past the willow grove and near the Zooks' lane, two cars pulled over. Several people got out carrying pocket cameras. I could spot out-of-state tourists almost instantly—by their throw-away cameras and the way they dressed. Especially the middle-aged men. Floral-patterned Bermuda-length shorts and knee socks with sandals. A dead giveaway.

One tourist had a video camera poised over his shoulder. I watched out of the corner of my eye as I walked along the opposite side of the road. The man with the camcorder started moving slowly across the road, zeroing in on the large wagon-wheel mailbox at the end of Zooks' lane. The closer I got to him, the more upset I became.

Then I heard Susie Zook calling my name. "Merry!" Somehow she had sneaked up on me, and was running toward me. She came barefoot, the narrow white tie strings on her kapp flying.

I shouted to her, "Quick, cover your face!"

It was too late, the heartless tourist aimed his camera right at my little friend.

I ran over and stood in front of her. "Take *my* picture if you have to."

"Move away there, Missy," he said, motioning me aside. "Just one more quick shot of the little Amish girl won't hurt anything."

I felt Susie's arms slip around my waist. And for one fleeting moment I remembered another day, another time, when Faithie had put her arms around me this way.

We had been posing for pictures while riding a white pony. It was our seventh birthday, and Faithie was terribly frightened. She'd clung to me, with her arms around my waist. . . .

"Go away!" I yelled at the tourist. "These people are not zoo animals. They're human beings!"

The man lowered his camera, staring at me. He reached into the pocket of his floral-patterned Bermudas and pulled out a wad of dollar bills. "Well, here, maybe this'll change your mind."

Susie's little arms tightened around me.

"Go away, please!" I said. But the man kept coming toward us. Closer . . . and closer.

Be strong and courageous. Do not be afraid.

Susie and I inched backward a few steps at a time, but there was no convincing this guy. He wasn't just a rude tourist—he was downright mean!

Just then, I saw a jazzy red sports car flying down SummerHill, headed right for the cameraman. The way the car zigzagged on the road was enough to scare tourists

76

out of the county—right out of their Bermuda shorts!

"Yee-ikes!" I cried, pointing. "That's our neighbor. She can't drive worth beans!"

The man jumped the ditch and dashed to the other side of the road, wearing a look of terror. Not to be defeated, Old Hawk Eyes bore down on him.

It was clear as anything—Ruby Spindler was up to her old spying tricks. Somehow she'd seen exactly what was going on out here. She had come to rescue us!

Abruptly, she braked her car, sending billowy clouds of dust into the air. Then, jumping out of the driver's seat, the old lady—with cell phone in hand—ran over to the guy with the camcorder. "Look-ee here, Mister," she squawked. "I don't know what yer business is, but as far as I can tell, you've been trepassing on private property." She glanced over at me, still hiding Susie. "Now I'm tellin' you—git!"

She backed up her words by dialing 911, reporting a harassment inches away from the tourist. It was as in-your-face as you get! And by the time she started to give pertinent information, the intruders had sped off down SummerHill. Long gone.

Susie crept out from behind me. "You saved us," she cried. "Oh, Old Hawk—"

"Uh . . . Miss Spindler, you were amazing," I interrupted.

"How's every little thing here now?" she asked Susie, leaning over to shake her hand. "Are you gonna be all right, darlin'?"

Susie nodded. "They were making *Schpott* of me, jah?"

"Not anymore, they won't make fun," Ruby Spindler said. "Not anymore, no indeedy!"

I stared in amazement at Old Hawk Eyes. Everyone knew she was a full-fledged busybody, but there was clearly another side to her. A very caring, almost parental side. I could hardly wait to report this aspect of her personality to Dad.

Much later, after the tourist ordeal was behind us, Mom decided to serve a light supper outside in the gazebo. Dad had slept the afternoon away, and Mom, fresh from her long walk and a shower, carried out a huge tray of chicken-salad sandwiches. There was potato salad made my favorite way with diced dill pickles, and a strawberry Jell-O mold with peaches hiding inside. Dad had to have his iced tea in a giant-sized tumbler, so I ran indoors for more ice and a pitcherful of tea.

I told my family about the adventure—about hiding Susie from the tourists and discovering the nurturing side to Miss Spindler. "It was actually scary there for a while," I said. "Old Hawk Eyes saved the day."

Skip snickered. "Man, what a snoop!"

"I have no idea how she does it—how she sees so far."

"It's gotta be some high-powered telescope set up in her bedroom," Skip said, pointing at her house in the distance. "Hey, we should all wave at her right now and freak her out."

"Skip Hanson, don't you dare!" Mom reprimanded.

"Don't worry," he said, reaching for three sandwich halves. "But I bet anything she's watching us."

I stole a glance at the old house. Wondering . . .

We bowed our heads for prayer. And while Dad

blessed the food, I prayed silently for Lissa.

Later, during dessert, Susie Zook showed up at the gazebo. "Can Merry play?" she asked my mom.

"Of course," Mom said, winking at me. "As soon as she's finished cleaning up the kitchen."

"I'll do the dishes," Dad volunteered. "You two run along."

I spied the canning jars in Susie's hands. "Are we going to catch fireflies again tonight?"

"Lightning bugs," she insisted, grinning. One of her front teeth was missing.

Skip must've noticed, too. "Hey, looks like the tooth fairy's coming to your house tonight!"

Susie looked puzzled. "Tooth fairy?"

"Oh, yeah," Skip said, scrunching up his face at me, trying to get me to bail him out.

"Tooth fairies aren't real," I began. "They're just pretend, like . . ." I paused, trying to think who on earth might make the connection in her Amish mind.

"Ever hear of Santa Claus?" Skip chimed in, getting himself in even deeper.

Susie frowned. "Ach, Santa Claus is worldly. Is the tooth fairy his dentist?"

Not one of us laughed, although I could tell by the way Dad looked down quickly, stirring his iced tea, that he was mighty close to it.

"Maybe we oughta just go catch some fireflies," I said, heading for the side yard with her.

"You mean lightning bugs, jah?"

"Jah." The word just slipped out, and I smiled to myself without turning around to see Mom's expression. She was probably worried sick that the Zooks were getting their hooks into me.

ELEVEN

We hurried down SummerHill Lane, then Susie had the idea to walk in the ditch that ran along the road. "We can hide in there and jump up and catch 'um," she announced, referring to her beloved bugs.

"Good idea." I crouched down in the grassy ditch, playing her little girl games—the kind of games Faithie and I had played so long ago. Kneeling down in the grassy area where wild strawberry vines grew—thick and beautiful—I pretended to be as young as my little friend.

One after another, the fireflies twinkled and came within catching distance. Occasionally, I caught one. Other times, they'd blink at me and disappear.

"Fourteen . . . fifteen . . . sixteen . . ." I heard Susie counting as she put the bugs inside her glass jar.

I thought of her grandfather's poem and stared at the fire-red sky. *Dusk comes wearing red satin.*

The tourists were out like flies tonight. Cars everywhere. Some of them pulled off to watch the Pennsylvania sunset. Others drove by slowly. Most of them never even noticed Susie and me creeping along in the ditch beside the road. *Dusk comes soft on tiptoes.*

Susie darted out onto the road to run after one hard-to-catch bug. She jumped into the air with her glass jar. A look of delight danced across her face. "I caught it, Merry! I caught it!"

I began to chant the firefly poem. "Come one, come all, to the firefly ball. Dance with 'um, laugh with 'um, run straight and tall."

Susie joined in, reciting the poem with me. "Come one, come all, to the firefly ball," she repeated in a sing-songy voice. "Dance with 'um . . ." She ran across the road without looking.

"Susie!" I called to her as a car *whooshed* past. "Didn't you see that car? Please, be careful." I hurried across the road and hugged her.

That's when I saw the tears. Big, round tears rolled down her angel face. "I smashed one by accident," she said. "I musta not caught it right."

I looked down at her hand. The firefly lay still in her palm, its light still glowing steadily.

"Don't worry," I said, comforting her.

"Did it feel the pain?" she asked.

"Probably not too much."

"I hope not." Still holding the dead firefly, she sat down and stared at the mass of twinkles in her jar.

I thought of Faithie as I watched my little friend. At six and a half, *she* had been full of questions, too. Always trying to understand nature and how things worked in God's scheme of things.

"We could go to my house and have lemonade." I sat down in the grass next to her, trying to get her mind off the smashed firefly. "Would you like that?"

"I wanna get a whole jarful tonight," she insisted, wiping tears off her cheeks.

I knew she needed time to calm down. So we admired our gleaming jars and said Grandfather Zook's poem again. "Come one, come all, to the firefly ball. Dance with 'um, laugh with 'um, run straight and tall."

We tried to remember the verses, but got all mixed up. Susie remembered the part about dusk wearing honeysuckle, and we leaned our heads back and breathed in the sweetness around us.

"Why do ya think God made lightning bugs, Merry?"

"Why do *you* think He did?"

"I'm gonna find out," she whispered, leaning close. "Levi snuck me some library books. He read some of the pages to me and told me it's good to be a thinker."

"Levi's right," I said. "It's good to think and ask questions."

"Mam and Dat say not."

I was silent, amazed at her perception of things.

"I ask the Lord questions sometimes," she said. "When I pray."

"You do?"

"Jah, every day when I'm doin' chores. Levi's the one who taught me how to pray to Jesus."

I felt warm and good hearing Levi's name linked with the Lord's. My Amish boyfriend was turning into a regular missionary!

Dusk had descended and the area was thick with dancing lights—more than I'd ever remembered seeing. With the darkness came less traffic, and I was glad to reclaim our peaceful strip of road.

"How's Rachel doing?" I asked. "Is she still mad at me?"

Susie took a deep breath. "Levi was talkin' to her out in the barn early. Somethin' 'bout you and her still bein' friends."

"That's good."

Susie stood up. "Rachel's real stubborn sometimes. I asked her, but she wouldn't even come one, come all, to the firefly ball."

"Did she know I would be coming, too?"

"Maybe."

So, Rachel was still holding a grudge. If only I could make her see that Levi's interest in the Bible and other things was his own doing. Not mine.

I followed Susie to a honeysuckle bush off the road. She picked some blossoms and put them inside her canning jar. "Lightning bugs like nectar."

I laughed. "Your firefly books say that, right?"

"I can't read yet, but Levi's teachin' me how."

"You'll be in the first grade soon," I said.

She nodded enthusiastically. "Come fall." She wandered back onto the road and squatted there, ready to catch another firefly.

A group of them flew past me—right in front of my nose—lighting up simultaneously. A duet. Maybe they were twins!

I ran after them, determined to have the twin fireflies together inside my canning jar. Safely together. I followed them as they flitted and fluttered toward the willow grove, alluring me with their matching lights.

"I'll be right back!" I called over my shoulder to Susie.

"Hurry," her little voice floated back to me.

I raced after the twosome.

Dance with 'um, laugh with 'um. Run straight and tall.

I reached up, stretching with all my might . . . and captured them. A triumph!

Quickly, I headed back through the grove of graceful trees. I couldn't wait to tell my little friend.

Susie Zook . . .

How truly terrific it was having someone like her in my life. She'd come along just when I needed her. And even though it was hard to admit to myself, she was actually beginning to fill Faithie's shoes in her own unique way. Well, not exactly, but very, very close.

I quickened my pace. A car's headlights shone just beyond the crest of the hill. I called to Susie. "Get off the road!"

A cold fear gripped me as I realized she was facing away from the car. She hadn't heard my warning.

"Sus-ee-ee!"

Dust was flying from the tires as the car sped down the narrow road.

I cupped my hands over my mouth and screamed. "Susie! A car's coming!"

The air had a strange smell to it. Like the way it smells right after a lightning strike.

Everything happened so fast. Loud, squealing brakes. The crash of a glass jar against the hood. And the sickening thud . . .

My heart pounded as I flew to her. My little friend . . .

my adorable playmate. Susie lay as still as death in the
soft, grassy ditch beside SummerHill Lane.

I knelt over her, sobbing. "Susie . . . Susie . . . oh
please, please don't die!" My jarful of fireflies rolled out
of my hand and into the grass.

The driver came running over. "Is she alive?" I heard
a low, choked sound and knew he was weeping. "I didn't
see her! I didn't—"

"Run, get help!" I shouted. "My father's a doctor." I
pointed to our house up the lane. "Go to that house and
call an ambulance! Quick!"

He left his car parked in the road with its flashers going. I could hear his desperate footsteps as I put my face
down next to Susie's, listening for her breathing. "Can
you hear me?" I whispered.

No response.

I touched her wrist gently, searching for a pulse. But
my own heart was pounding so hard, I couldn't be sure.
With trembling fingers, I picked up her white prayer cap.
It had fallen onto the grass beside her. Something in me
longed to place it back on her head where it belonged.
But I held it close to my heart instead, fearful of moving
her.

Be strong and courageous. Do not be afraid.

"Oh, help us, dear Jesus. Please help us!" I prayed.

Then I heard anxious footsteps pounding down the
Zooks' lane. "Merry! What's happened?"

It was Levi. He knelt beside me and touched his sister's hand tenderly.

"A car hit her," I managed to say. "I can't tell if
she's—"

"I . . . I'll call an ambulance," he stammered.

"Someone already has."

"Then I must tell Dat and Mam," he said. And he dashed off toward the Zook farmhouse.

Up the road, my father and Skip were running toward us. "Susie, hang on . . . don't give up. Help is coming," I said into her ear.

Then I touched her left wrist again, and when I did, her fingers opened, revealing the dead firefly in her cool palm. Its steady light was still shining.

In the dark I began to cry silently. For Susie, and for myself.

TWELVE

Still clutching Susie's prayer cap, I stepped back to make room for Dad and his medical bag. Skip brought a blanket and covered Susie's tiny body.

Within minutes, Abe and Esther Zook came running with Levi and the rest of the children. Rachel came over to where I was standing. She was crying. "Didja see it happen?" she asked.

"I tried to warn her . . . it happened so fast." I reached for Rachel's hand. I was shaking. "I would've done anything . . . anything . . . to stop this from happening." I could hardly talk, my teeth chattered so hard.

"I know, Merry. I don't blame you." She turned to me and we clung to each other.

Then I gave Susie's white kapp to her. "It fell off. . . ." I tried, but I couldn't say more.

Rachel seemed to understand and held her sister's prayer covering almost reverently in both hands.

The Zook grandparents arrived on the scene using their canes to steady themselves. I shivered even more when I saw them. As I inched backward, farther and farther away, I covered my face with my hands, shutting out the horror.

The frantic wail of an ambulance rang out in the distance. I knew it wouldn't be long till Susie would be speeding off to the hospital.

Abe and Esther hovered over their daughter looking solemn and sober in the light of an eerie set of headlights. I could hear Dad's calm, professional voice explaining that he had begun to treat Susie for shock symptoms, but that her pulse was very faint. I shuddered to think of my firefly friend—so energetic, alive, and spunky just minutes ago—now so lifeless.

Esther dropped to her knees, leaning over the still form of her baby daughter. She rocked back and forth as though travailing, but not a sound escaped her lips.

Mom came running down SummerHill, along with the driver of the car. The man was around Dad's age, and he looked thoroughly shaken. Once he almost fell as he made his way to the scene of the accident.

The closer he got, the more I wanted to lash out at him. Let him know I hoped he had to pay, and pay dearly, for this truly horrible thing.

Mom came over to me and held me close. "Oh, honey," she whispered. "Honey."

My knees felt weak and I nearly collapsed. Dad rushed over and had me lie down in the grass, my head cradled in Mom's lap.

And then, the ambulance arrived. Lights swirled round and round, casting reddish shadows on the trees surrounding us.

In the darkness, I thought how it would be to take

Susie's place. For me to be the one dying instead. For me to be going to heaven . . . to Faithie.

Tears rolled down my face and slid into my ears. But I let them fall, wishing something would block out the sound of Susie's body being lifted onto a stretcher and into the ambulance, its doors closing heavily. I trembled uncontrollably and was only vaguely aware of someone covering me with a blanket.

Mom's gentle voice was somewhere above me. "I'm here, Merry," she said. And then came Dad's strong arms, lifting me up and carrying me home.

❧   ❧

I tossed and turned between my sheets, reliving the accident, calling out to Susie in the night. I even dreamed the whole thing—except in my dream, she'd heard my warning. And was safe.

Close to midnight, I fell into a deep, sorrowful sleep.

The next morning, I couldn't remember the details of my dream. I knew I'd been catching fireflies with Susie and calling . . . calling. But nothing else was clear. And try as I might, I couldn't recall the outcome.

The longer I lay there, the more restless I became. I checked the time on my blue-striped wall clock. Already ten o'clock!

I got out of bed, eager for news of Susie. Was she alive? Had she survived the first critical hours?

I grabbed my robe and stumbled into the hallway, calling for Mom.

"Downstairs," she answered, meeting me at the bottom of the back stairs leading to the kitchen.

"How's Susie?" I stood there stiff as a soldier, bracing myself for the worst.

"Come, sit down." Mom guided me over to the table.

I felt suddenly guilty for sleeping while my friend was shut away in the hospital. Maybe dying.

"Your dad went to the hospital last night after we got you settled. He stayed through the night with Susie and her parents." Her voice was thick with concern. "Honey, it doesn't look good."

My throat felt cottony, and I wished I could go back to bed, to sleep, and have all this be just a bad dream.

She reached over and touched my hand. "Susie's in a coma."

My heart sank. "A coma?"

She nodded, a hint of tears in her eyes.

"I want to see her," I whispered.

"I knew you would, so I fixed some pancakes. I can warm them up right away for you."

I shook my head. "I'm not hungry, Mom."

"But you nearly fainted last night," she said, getting up. "You ought to try and eat something. For nourishment."

"Okay, but just a little."

I watched her slip into a hostess mode and hurry to the fridge, where she located a pitcher of orange juice. She poured it thoughtfully into a small juice glass and brought it over to me.

"Thanks," I said in a daze.

"The Zooks were so kind to your father last night," she offered. "They never questioned anything in the ER. Their only concern was for Susie."

"I'm not surprised," I said. "They trust Dad. And most of all, the providence of God."

She set the microwave for reheat and put a plate of pancakes inside. "Your dad said Levi was a big help, filling out forms for the nurses, and in general handling the whole situation amazingly well."

There was so much she wasn't saying. I knew it by the look in her eyes. She desperately wanted to have the Amish conversion conversation now.

"Mom, the Zooks aren't trying to convert me, I promise you. There *are* some things going on with Levi, though." I sighed. "I just don't want to talk now."

She put the orange juice back in the fridge. "It can wait." She forced a smile.

Silence came from Mom. But I could feel the tension between us.

I got up and looked out the back window. The gazebo reminded me of Levi. He was so mature, much more settled than I'd ever dreamed. Settled and now tremendously strong. He wasn't nearly the flirt, either. That aspect of him was actually refreshing. I had to admit, the new Levi was more intense. Self-directed, too.

I wondered how God looked at our lives. Knowing the end from the beginning the way He did. Knowing whether or not Levi would wait for me to grow up. And whether or not I'd want him to.

I turned away from the window. Now wasn't the time to be thinking about Levi. So much was at stake. Susie's life was on the line.

One pancake was all I could eat. Thank goodness, Mom didn't coax for more. It was clear she wasn't herself. I wondered if Susie's accident had jolted her—forcing her to reevaluate her relationship with me.

❧　❧

We stopped in at the Zooks' before heading to Lancaster General Hospital. I got out of the car and went inside, asking if anyone wanted to ride along.

Grandfather Zook stood up and took his cane, looking relieved. "I'll go in with ya. Denki for thinking of us."

Levi and Aaron were covering the chores for their father. Rachel, Nancy, and Ella Mae helped, too. By the looks of things, Grandma Zook had taken over all kitchen duties.

Poor Grandfather. He'd been twiddling his thumbs, not knowing what to do with himself. "Yous are a Godsend," he said, getting into the backseat of our car.

"Glad to help," Mom said. She had an uncanny ability to pull herself together. Mom talked softly with him, filling him in on the latest hospital information from Dad as she drove us toward Lancaster.

I shut out their talk, remembering back to Faithie's diagnosis of cancer. The outlook had been bleak right from the start. The cancer had crept up on all of us—taking a head start on everything medically possible. In eight short months she was gone.

Gone!

I trembled at the thought. Would we have to go through the same trauma and grief again? Wasn't it enough to lose Faithie? Wasn't it?

I felt hot—caged in—sitting here in the front seat of Mom's expensive car. At the red light, I put my hand on the door handle and, in my mind, jumped out. I imagined running down Lime Street—all the way to the hospital.

The weather was beastly hot and sultry, as though a thundershower was imminent. A sizzling Fourth.

Even though Mom had the air-conditioner going full blast, I was perspiring to beat the band. The sheer thought of seeing little Susie in a hospital bed frightened me.

As it turned out, Abe Zook had to do some fast talking to let Mom and me in to see Susie at all. He called us cousins, which we were, only very distant ones. The nurse in charge eyed us suspiciously, probably because we didn't look one bit plain.

Abe and Esther Zook had been taking turns in the intensive-care unit off and on since last night. Abe looked washed out, exhausted. Esther, too. Someone at the hospital had taken Levi home in the wee hours.

Tears came to Esther's eyes when she saw Grandfather Zook shuffling down the hall, his cane in hand. The three of them stood in a huddle, speaking in Pennsylvania Dutch quietly as they shared their grief, felt one another's pain, and, by their faces, the hopelessness of it all.

That's when Mom encouraged me to go inside to see Susie. I felt a lump in my throat. It choked me so that I could hardly breathe as I stood at the foot of her bed.

Do not be afraid or discouraged. . . .

White sheets draped the bed, matching Susie's pale face. Her braids had been wound around her head in the typical little-girl style, and her white net bonnet covered her small, round head.

I studied her eyelids, hoping they might flutter open. "Oh, Susie," I spoke to her, trying my best not to cry. "I know you can't see me, but I'm here. I miss you." I took a deep breath for courage. "I know you'd rather be anywhere else but here. And believe me, I wish you weren't here either."

I longed for some kind of signal. Something to let me know she could hear—that she was listening. But there was nothing at all. Not the slightest movement of her fingers or her eyelids.

Nothing.

Slowly, I walked around to the side of her bed. I touched her left hand gently. The hand that had held the smashed firefly last night.

"I'm going out tonight . . . to catch fireflies. Hurry and get well so you can come with me," I said with absolutely no hope that she would ever come to another firefly ball.

I stared at the monitors everywhere and at the curtains, pulled shut. This place was like a morgue. Except for one thing. There was a *live* body in this room. A living, breathing person!

Dad had always said, "Where there's life, there's hope," and I clung to that. Susie might've died last night, but she was alive, her heart beating. Breathing on her own!

So much to be thankful for.

I thought of the firefly poem—the one Grandfather Zook had written. "Night of the Fireflies," I said out loud. "Come one, come all, to the firefly ball. Dance with 'um, laugh with 'um. Run straight and tall."

I looked at Susie—really looked at her. She was somewhere inside that lifeless body; I knew it. Her light was still shining. Same as the firefly she'd accidentally smashed. Shining steadily . . . telling us not to give up. To keep believing that she would run and laugh again. That she would chase fireflies again.

But no one else, not her family and not the nurses, seemed quite as hopeful. Dad came up on one of his breaks. He checked her chart and reaffirmed the grim outlook. Susie was in a deep coma.

"Can she hear anything?" I asked.

"Sometimes comatose patients have keen hearing; they're aware of their surroundings. My guess is that Susie can probably hear the voices of those she loves."

"My voice, too?"

Dad kissed my cheek. "Perhaps."

I stayed all day, rotating turns with Susie's mother, father, and grandfather. I used the Gideon Bible from the drawer in Susie's hospital room to read passages from the Psalms out loud.

Grandfather Zook had his firefly poem with him, and while he waited for his visits, he worked on creating the last verse. When the words didn't fit just right, we would talk, sharing special memories of Susie.

We weren't being morbid or anything. Actually, our time together was very sweet . . . and touching. Fond memories of Susie kept us going. Kept us hoping.

THIRTEEN

A Fourth of July without fireworks. No hot dogs or corn on the cob. No root beer floats.

I was content to sit at Susie's bedside a few minutes at a time, reading Psalms to her and praying out loud—making sure the light inside her kept shining.

"Here's a good one—Psalm Ninety-One," I said, settling down for another Bible-reading session. "It's one of my favorites. 'He who dwells in the shelter of the Most High will rest in the shadow of the Almighty.' "

I paused, thinking about the sheltering willows in our secret place—the willow grove. "Remember how bright our jars of fireflies were in the willow trees? Well, I guess you could say the willows are like the shelter in this psalm. Can you picture yourself being sheltered there, Susie—safe in Jesus? He is the Almighty."

I looked at her as I spoke, hoping, praying for a response. Anything.

Undaunted, I picked up the Bible again and continued to read. "I will say of the Lord, 'He is my refuge and my fortress, my God, in whom I trust.' "

Then, as I did after every short session, I repeated her

grandfather's poem, "Night of the Fireflies."

"Come one, come all, to the firefly ball. Dance with 'um, laugh with 'um. Run straight and tall."

❧　　❧

Mom left the hospital around noon, taking Abe Zook home en route to our house. He'd gone to catch forty winks, planning to return to the hospital with the rest of the Zook children after the last milking. And they came into Lancaster together, piled up in the usual way in their horse and buggy.

Levi, Rachel, Nancy, Ella Mae, and Aaron all gathered around their sister. They were allowed to stay as long as they were quiet.

After supper, Curly John, the oldest Zook boy, and Sarah, his young bride, came to visit. Sarah was starting to look as though she was expecting a baby. The new little Zook was scheduled to arrive in mid-November.

When the young couple came out of Susie's room, they had tears in their eyes but no other display of emotion. Quietly, they stood talking with Abe and Esther in the hall, and then there was a long period of silence.

It was difficult for everyone to see the young girl, once so lively and vibrant, in this anguishing, dismal state—hanging somewhere between life and death.

My dad had agreed to take me home when he got off work after supper. I felt truly blessed to have spent this day—off and on, of course—with my friend. Our time together had been nothing like our jaunts around the farm chasing fireflies, but it had been special. Special beyond words.

The scriptures and the prayers had touched the very heart of me. I could only hope they had reached Susie, too.

Later, Levi talked his parents and grandfather into going home for some rest. "Try and get a good night's sleep," he urged them. Then, to put their minds at ease, "The doctor will call Merry's house if Susie takes a turn for the worse."

"Or if there's good news," I added cheerfully.

Esther and Abe finally agreed and took Grandfather and their brood home for the night—in a mighty cramped buggy.

Much later, when the only sounds from Susie's room were distant pops and explosions of shooting fireworks, Levi and I had another private talk.

"I've read nearly ten psalms to her today." I showed Levi the Bible I'd found.

He cast a tender look at his sister. "Susie loves the Bible, jah," he said, returning his gaze to me. "Do ya think God's Word will heal her?"

"One-hundred-percent-amen sure!" I said. "In fact, there's a verse in the Psalms about it."

"Ach, let's find it." Levi went to the drawer and pulled out the black Gideon Bible. "Which psalm do ya think it is?"

"Check in the back—there's a small concordance."

I peeked over his shoulder as he searched under the word *healed*. And, sure enough, there it was.

"Psalms one hundred and seven, verse twenty," I said.

Levi's face lit up when he found it. "Here's the whole verse. 'He sent forth his word and healed them; he rescued them from the grave.' "

Levi looked at me, his face shining. "Oh, Merry, it's a wonderful-gut verse! We gotta keep on reading God's Word to her!"

It was a startling remark, especially because it seemed to indicate that he thought Susie could hear us.

"My Dad says that unconscious people are aware of loved ones surrounding them—that what we say should be positive and uplifting," I told him.

I went to sit in the soft chair near the window across the room. Levi kept standing, though, leaning against the windowsill—the Bible still open in his hands. He began to read several more verses from the psalm.

From my chair, I surveyed Susie's tiny form covered with hospital-white sheets and a lightweight blanket. When Levi stopped reading, I asked, "Do you think she knows we're here together, you and I?"

"Betcha she does." He smiled, closing the Bible. "Ya know, Susie's wanted you for a sister of sorts ever since I can remember."

I grinned, enjoying the idea of being someone's big sister. Actually, Susie and I *had* been like sisters for the past several days. Sisters . . . and playmates.

"I'm going to come see her every day till she wakes up," I announced. "And I don't care how long it takes!"

Levi was silent, and by the look on his face, troubled.

"What's wrong?" I asked. "Don't you believe she'll—"

"Merry, *please*. This has nothin' to do with believin'. Sometimes God's plans are different than ours. Sometimes . . ." His voice trailed off.

"Well, I won't give up hope."

"But ya hafta prepare yourself for the other possibility, ya know."

"But I thought—"

"I believe God heals the sick, jah—but *you* know as well as I do that sometimes the healing comes by lettin' a person die."

I squinted my eyes nearly shut. "What are you saying?"

"It's just that . . ." He paused, having trouble getting the words out. "Susie . . . uh, might not make it."

"Better not be saying that in *this* room!" I insisted. "If Susie's listening, which I'm sure she is, you oughta be saying good, truthful, powerful things. Things that'll stimulate her mind. Things to make her want to wake up."

Levi frowned. "Don't hide your head in the sand, Merry. I would be so sorry for ya to be disappointed."

"I won't be, you'll see!" And I leaped out of my chair and left the room without saying goodbye to him.

Or to Susie.

❧   ❧

On the ride home, Levi asked my dad many questions about comatose states. He seemed hungry to know as much about Susie's condition as possible. Still, I was upset at the abrupt change in his attitude. Did he believe the Bible or not?

Dad was kind enough to answer Levi's medical questions, even though I could see he was fairly wiped out from having been up all last night. On top of that, he'd worked the ER all day.

Finally, when we made the turn onto SummerHill, all of us grew quiet. I turned my attention to the scenery outside.

Susie's lightning bugs were out in droves—almost as thick as I'd seen them last night. The night of the accident . . . the night of the fireflies.

I thought of Grandfather Zook's poem—the references to dusk wearing red satin and honeysuckle. My mind drifted back. How uncanny that there had been a fire-red sunset like a red satin gown. And the night air had been heavily sprinkled with the sweet smell of honeysuckle. Susie had even stopped to pick several blossoms!

I closed my eyes, refusing to look at the scene of the accident as we came near it. When we passed it, I caught Levi's sad eyes staring at me. He wasn't just sad—Levi was ticked. We'd had our first fight. Over a life and death issue. Over Susie's life, and whether she would come out of the coma, or die and go on to heaven.

As I looked at Levi's grim face, I couldn't tell whether the pain he was feeling was stronger for Susie, or for me.

FOURTEEN

I told Dad I wanted to sit outside for a while after we arrived home. "I need some time alone."

"You sure, kiddo?" he asked.

I nodded, trying to ignore the sweet fragrance around me. "I'm sure."

"Well then, take your time." He left me sitting outside on the gazebo steps.

As I looked up into the evening sky, I wondered where Susie really was. Oh, I knew where her *body* was. But she was unconscious, so where was her mind? And what about her soul—the spirit of her?

Susie's most essential natural reflexes were working without artificial means—her heart beating, her lungs breathing. It was her mind that was shut off. And the more I thought about it, the more determined I was to find a way to awaken her. To bring her back—all of her!

I decided not to catch fireflies after all. There was thunder in the distance, and it was getting late. Besides that, I was tired from the events of the past two days.

I called for my cats, wondering if they were hiding in

their usual spot under the gazebo steps. "Lily White? Are you under there?"

Abednego, the cat who was usually missing, showed up first. He padded up to me, his persistent meowing getting to be a little much.

"Okay, okay. I know you're glad to see me, little boy." Abednego wasn't so little anymore. In fact, he was downright fat. Probably due to the rich, raw cow's milk from Zooks' dairy. "I should put you on a diet!"

He didn't appreciate that comment and arched his back in disgust. My tone of voice had probably offended him. He was terribly sensitive but *very* smart. In fact, all four of my cats were super intelligent. They just didn't understand English.

Minutes later, I was joined by the rest of the feline delegation of the Hanson household. Lily White, the youngest, led the pack. She was petite and wore a regal coat of white. Shadrach and Meshach were golden-haired brothers, younger siblings to Abednego. I'd noticed recently that Lily and Abednego had been viciously vying for my attention.

Lily was the new cat on the block, still attempting to establish her worth, while the three Hebrew felines had been around for years.

A gust of wind took me by surprise. Quickly, I gestured to my cat quartet, informing them of the impending storm. "Let's get inside before it pours," I said, gathering Lily White in my arms. Abednego took notice and ran under the gazebo, having a temper tantrum.

Thunder rolled over head.

"Aw, c'mon, little boy," I called to him. "You don't

want to get caught in a thunderstorm. Please come."

I squatted down, peering under the gazebo, still holding Lily White.

Abednego was stubborn and going to play his little game. I was pretty sure if I put Lily down and *then* coaxed him, he'd come out in a flash. But I was too tired emotionally and physically to plead with the spoiled old feline, so I scrambled into the house just as lightning lit up the sky.

"Merry," Mom said, looking concerned as she glanced out the back-door window. "I was just coming to get you. There's a severe thunderstorm warning out for Lancaster County. We just heard it on the radio."

I put Lily White down. "Abednego's still out there!"

Skip looked up from his plate of pie and ice cream. "What's *his* problem?"

"Probably jealous." I turned around, staring out the window with Mom, upset at the way Abednego had ignored me. Didn't he know by now that I wanted the best for him? That I only wanted him to be safe?

I went to the fridge in search of sandwich fixings.

"Jealousy is as cruel as the grave," Mom stated.

Her words stung my heart. "What?" I said, even though I'd heard her just fine.

"Abednego's competing for all he's worth," she said. "Lily White makes him mad because she moved in on his territory."

I knew all that. But it was the "cruel as the grave" part that I couldn't get out of my mind.

Mom insisted on warming up something for Dad and me to eat, even though I was content with making a sandwich. "You've had a stressful day," she said, coming over to the counter. "You have to keep up your strength."

Dad sighed, running his hand over his prickly chin. "I could use a good hot shower and shave."

It was obvious that Dad had already filled Mom in on Susie's condition. During the course of the meal, neither of them offered a word about her recovery. That bothered me. Was I the only one holding out hope?

After supper, Mom said she and Skip would clean up the kitchen. I was relieved. There was no way I'd survive even a half hour of chitchat with them. Everyday living seemed so mundane and unimportant when it came to eternal questions about life and death.

                        ge   ge

The next day I got up early and rode into town with Dad. I was going to spend the whole day with Susie.

Mom had made an enormous sack lunch for me, and when the nurse saw me brown-bagging it, she let me use their staff refrigerator. I was all set.

Rachel and her mother arrived soon after I did, and we traded off visits the way we had yesterday. I read all of Psalm One Hundred and Seven to Susie without interruption from nurses or other visitors, emphasizing the part about being rescued from the grave. Then, as my five minutes drew to a close, I recited "Night of the Fireflies," ending with the refrain.

"Come one, come all, to the firefly ball. Dance with 'um, laugh with 'um. Run straight and tall."

When the doctor came in for morning rounds, he solemnly indicated to Esther that Susie seemed to be drifting deeper into the coma. Truly horrible news!

However, because of that fact, Esther, Rachel, and I were allowed to stay in the room for longer periods of time.

There was only one problem with that—I couldn't conduct my visit with Susie the way I had been. That worried me because I was sure my interaction with Susie was helping. Not that I had anything solid to go on—no flutters of movement or deeper breathing it was just a strong feeling.

Esther Zook scooted her chair up close to her daughter's hospital bed, which had been slightly elevated for the doctor's examination. She wore a black dress with a gray apron and the white prayer bonnet. Holding Susie's hand in hers, she closed her eyes in silent prayer. For nearly an hour she sat there without moving. Without speaking.

I was frustrated. She needed to be talking to Susie! How could I tactfully tell her?

After lunch, more and more Amish and Mennonite relatives began showing up, filing in and out of Susie's room, some staying as long as fifteen minutes at a time. Others came in briefly to greet Esther and Rachel. Several of Susie's aunts and uncles recognized me and kindly came over to the window where I sat. They were warm and sincere in their hellos and thank-yous, but I was one-hundred-percent-amen sure they could've done miraculous things if they had simply gone over to Susie's bed and spoken to *her*.

Word had spread through the Amish community about the accident, and by late afternoon the trickle of plain visitors had become a steady stream.

I needed a break from the funeral-like atmosphere and the "silent treatment" they were giving Susie. It seemed as though they were coming to pay their respects!

There was only one good thing about me being here today, I decided. Rachel and I might have an opportunity to work out our problems over Levi. Maybe . . .

Like the longtime friends we were, she and I settled down into the soft, green leather sofa in the private waiting room down the hall. People with family members in ICU could use the room as a place to relax or wait for word from a doctor or surgeon. Rachel and I used the cozy place, surrounded by fake greenery, to begin our peace talks.

"I think I understand why ya wanted Levi to talk to me," she began hesitantly.

"You do?"

"I never meant for Levi's decision to make us enemies." She folded her hands in her lap. "He's always been interested in finding out answers to things. Never content to take no for an answer."

I nodded. "Levi can be stubborn sometimes, but maybe this is a good thing."

Rachel looked a bit surprised. "I don't see how that can be."

I covered my mouth with my hand, thinking, choosing my words carefully. "Levi says that the name of a church or religion doesn't count for much. It's the way a person lives, the way he walks with God that matters."

Rachel's blue eyes grew wide. But she didn't respond.

I sighed. How could I explain to her what Levi had

confided in me? How much did she know about his plans to attend Bible school?

"Well, I know ya didn't have anything to do with Levi's decision to become a preacher," she said softly. "He has lotsa Mennonite friends. They feel called to evangelize."

"How do your parents feel?"

She turned to face me for the first time, and I saw tears well up in her eyes. "Levi's not rebellious like he was. We've seen a change in him. It's for the better, jah."

"So he won't get kicked out or anything?"

"Dat says he can stay and farm as long as he likes."

I was glad to hear it, and even happier to know that Rachel and I were back on good terms.

Suddenly, Esther Zook came into the room, surrounded by her older sisters. She was leaning on them as though she was about to faint.

"Mam!" Rachel hurried over to help her. "Was ist letz?"

"Ach, she's exhausted," one of Rachel's aunts explained, looking mighty worried as she fanned a handkerchief.

"She's plain worn out from all this," said the other aunt. "And I'm afraid there's bad news."

I cringed. I couldn't bear to hear it. Quietly, I excused myself.

FIFTEEN

I hurried down the hall to Susie's room and tiptoed inside. My eyes scanned the room. Empty!

My heart stood still. What if Susie had already gone to heaven?

I rushed to her bedside—forcing my eyes to focus on the heart monitor, relieved to see the IV still attached to her arm. Confused, I stood there surveying the situation. What *was* the bad news?

"Susie," I spoke to her. "I'm here to give you some good news. I believe God is going to make you well, and I have just the words to prove it."

I reached for the Bible in the small table beside her bed. "Listen to this." And I began to read out loud again from Psalm One Hundred and Seven, verse twenty. "He sent forth his word and healed them; he rescued them from the grave."

I read it again and again, feeling the intensity, the power of the words. Then I read the next psalm, and the next. I talked to her, recounting the many adventures we'd had together. I talked of the lovely poem her grandfather was writing and all the unfinished things in her life.

"Curly John and Sarah are expecting a baby sometime before Thanksgiving. You're going to be an aunt, Susie. An aunt at age seven! That's amazing, don't you think? I'm sure you'll want to hold your little niece or nephew— rock the baby to sleep sometimes. Show him . . . or her . . . how to catch lightning bugs." Tears stung my eyes.

I stopped to catch my breath, stroking her hand. I remembered the dead firefly with its shimmering tail. "Long before Curly John and Sarah's baby comes, you and I will be out catching lightning bugs again. As soon as you're up and out of here, we'll start. Is it a deal?"

I looked in the back of the Bible and found oodles of verses about light. Susie loved light. Especially her bugs.

I looked up every verse dealing with light. One after another I read them to her, sometimes adding my own two cents worth about the particular verse. Not embellishing it, just simply explaining it.

My voice was starting to wear out from all the reading, but I refused to stop.

Once, I actually thought her hand twitched. I couldn't be sure, though. I didn't want to stop and tell the others. I knew I was making progress here, and time was too precious to waste.

When it came time for supper, I didn't bother to eat, even though my dad had ordered food for me.

Rachel, with some strong assistance from her aunts, was able to talk her mother into going home for a nourishing meal and some much-needed rest. Levi and his grandfather would return later.

I was overjoyed about having more time with Susie. Now I could stimulate her brain to my heart's content—

with long chapters from the Bible. With heartfelt prayers for her recovery. With long, intimate talks about everything under the sun. And more.

The nurse came frequently to check monitors and Susie's temperature. The nurse was friendly, and I was encouraged that she didn't act as though I were in the way. She seemed to welcome my presence. Hours later, though, she looked surprised to see me still here.

"You must be a good friend of our little miss," she said while taking Susie's blood pressure.

"We're very close, almost like sisters."

The nurse smiled, then checked the amount of fluid left in the IV. "Susie is very lucky to have you."

"She's very special, and I'm not giving up," I told her. "I want to be right here when she wakes up!"

"Wouldn't that be wonderful?" she said.

Around eight o'clock, Levi and Grandfather Zook arrived. I was glad to see them and asked Levi to read the Bible or talk to Susie in Pennsylvania Dutch, hoping the familiar language might trigger something in her.

"Jah, I will," Levi said. "Good idea."

I was glad to hear the friendly ring in his voice. But I wondered how he felt about our former disagreement.

I sat in the chair next to the window while Levi spoke to his sister in their first language.

Next, Grandfather Zook took a turn. "Susie, my little one," he began. "I'm done writing your poem. Jah"—and here he nodded his head slowly—"my work is done."

He reached into his pocket and pulled out a folded page. "I have it right here if ya wanna give a listen."

I sat up, eager to hear the final verse, wondering if

Susie was excited about it, too—inside herself some-where.

"First, I brought somethin' for ya." He held up a glass canning jar filled with fireflies. With a slow sweep of his hand, he motioned for Levi to turn off the lights.

Gently, using the covers to prop it up, he placed the jar of Susie's beloved lightning bugs in front of her face. "There, child," I heard him whisper.

A lump caught in my throat as he stood there in the silence of the dim room, the shimmering glow of the fire-flies reflected on Susie's angel-white face.

Then Grandfather Zook began to read his newly com-pleted poem. " 'Tis the night of the fireflies, 'Tis the night of God's call. Dusk comes and is gone, and now . . ."

I held my breath listening to the poetic phrases.

"True light shines on us all."

My face was wet with tears as he began the familiar refrain. Quietly, I went to stand beside the old man, say-ing the rest of the poem with him.

"Come one, come all, to the firefly ball. Dance with 'um, laugh with 'um. Run straight and tall."

And again . . .

"Come one, come all, to the firefly ball. Fly with 'um, flit with 'um. Run straight and tall."

Levi's eyes appeared misty. But it was Grandfather's eyes that spilled over with tears. He shook his head slowly when I looked up at him, reassuring me that I shouldn't worry.

I reached up to touch his cheek, then put my arms around him. His weeping came softly without sobs. And I let my own tears fall unchecked.

SIXTEEN

Later, Levi suggested to his grandfather that they head home before it got late. But before they left, I asked Levi if we could talk in the hall. With Susie's door safely closed behind us, I whispered my secret to him about the slight twitch in Susie's hand.

"Ach! Are ya sure?" His eyes searched mine.

I shook my head. "I wish I could say for sure." I waited. "But I *do* have this strong feeling. . . ."

"I know whatcha mean." He looked at me thoughtfully. "I feel it, too."

"Oh, Levi, I'm so glad!" His blue eyes twinkled under the fluorescent lights, and for a second I honestly thought he was going to hug me.

Curious glances from the nurses' station told us we were drawing an audience. Levi pointed to the more private waiting area, where we went to talk things over. Our conversation centered around yesterday's tiff.

"I went home and read my Bible most all night," Levi began. "I found lotsa verses about healing." He paused reflectively.

"It's so strange and new to me, Merry. All my life, I

was taught that whatever happens is divinely ordered—
our fate. When our barn burned down, it was just supposed to be—we were suffering the wrath of God for the
whole community."

He took a deep breath. "When someone dies, we say,
'The Lord giveth and the Lord taketh away'—but I
wanna know that God hears the cries of His people. That
He is touched by our grief. That by our prayers we can
move the hand of the heavenly Father."

I looked at him, astounded. "Levi Zook, you sound
like a preacher!" His eyes were shining like the fireflies
Grandfather had brought for Susie.

"I'm believin' with ya for Susie," he said softly. "And
I'm sorry about getting in a huff about it before."

"Things are hard for all of us," I said. "No need to
apologize."

~ ~

After Levi left with his grandfather, I went back to
Susie's room. I started telling her the things Levi and I
had discussed.

"There are *two* of us now, Susie." I pushed the big,
comfortable chair over next to her bed. "Levi and I both
believe God's going to heal you . . . one of these days."

That's when I decided I wanted to sleep right there in
the enormous chair beside her bed. I wanted to fall asleep
talking to my friend.

Dad didn't put up much of a fuss when he came to
take me home, but I guess Mom thought it was ridiculous
when he called to tell her. "Your mother's concerned that
you're overdoing it," he said after hanging up.

"Tell her I'm fine. Honest." I went over to hug him.

"I can see that." He kissed my forehead. "The hospital only makes exceptions for spouses or close family members of patients.

"Aw, Daddy. Can't you clear it with the nurses?" I pleaded. "Please? I *have* to do this!"

"Don't get your hopes up about staying. I can't promise anything." He left me alone with Susie as he went to try to push his weight around.

I sat twiddling my thumbs, not sure what to do with my nervous energy. Praying silently, I hurried to the windows and peered out at the ink black sky. An array of twinkling lights mingled against the backdrop of darkness.

The moonless sky reminded me of Susie's coma— black and hopeless. But the city lights were like the fireflies still shining intermittently beside her in the canning jar. The light meant hope. Hope . . . and courage.

When Dad didn't return right away, I became nervous. What if the hospital wouldn't let me stay?

I went to Susie's bedside. I looked at the still, limp form that was her body. It was difficult seeing her like this. The Susie Zook *I* knew would've wanted to leap out of bed by now. She'd be chattering, too—about everything under the sun. That was the girl I was waiting for.

The door opened.

Dad was wearing a big, almost mischievous grin. "What do you need for the night?" he asked. "A pillow, maybe?"

"I can stay?" I ran to him. "Oh, thank you, thank you!"

"You're doing the patient a lot of good," he said. "The nurses said so."

"What's that mean?" My heart was pounding with excitement. "Is something new happening?"

He shook his head. "There's nothing new to report on Susie's condition, but look, see that color in her cheeks?" He went over to the bed and touched her face gently. "Just a hint of color."

We stood side by side looking at her.

"You're right," I said, picking up the small jar of fireflies. "Do you believe in miracles, Daddy?"

"Sure do."

"They happened in the Bible all the time." I kept staring at the lights inside the jar.

"Miracles can happen anytime. Sometimes when we least expect them."

Dad made sure I was comfortable—I had several pillows and a lightweight blanket—before he left. "I'll see you in the morning." He hugged me close. "You're a very courageous girl."

I sighed. "I sure hope Mom's not too upset."

"Don't worry," he said with a wink. "She'll be fine." Then he was gone.

I turned to Susie, still holding the jar filled with fireflies. "I'll be right back. I have to set your lightning bugs free."

I told the nurse at the nurses' station where I was going, then hurried to the elevators and down to the main level. Outside, I opened the lid.

"Come one, come all, to the firefly ball," I quoted Grandfather Zook's poem as the twinkly bugs flew out of the jar. "Dance with 'um, laugh with 'um. Run straight and tall."

Then I raced back inside. That's when I bumped into Lissa Vyner.

"Merry, hi!" She sounded excited to see me.

What was she doing here?

I had just pressed the elevator button. "Oh . . . hi." I remembered that I'd thought of calling her several times this week. Now I felt worse than ever because I hadn't.

"I . . . uh . . . really wanted to clear things up between us," I began, faltering a bit. "I wanted to talk to you about last Sunday—"

"Don't worry about it," she said. "Jon and I aren't going out anymore."

"You're *not?*"

She studied me for a moment. "Oh, Merry, I'm so sorry about your Amish friend. When I heard about Susie and everything, I wished I hadn't said all those things about you and . . . and them."

She stared at the numbers above the elevator door. When the door opened, we got on together. "That's why I'm here. We've been such good friends, until . . ." Her voice trailed off.

"Guys can get in the way sometimes," I said, still wondering if she suspected anything between Jon and me. "You'll have to come help me talk to Susie."

She looked at me with a blank expression. "I really didn't come to see her." She stepped off the elevator when the doors opened, and we walked together down the hallway to the waiting area.

I explained my ideas, strange as they sounded.

"Susie's in a coma, but I've been talking to her anyway. I'm trying to stimulate her brain."

"You have to do this?"

"I don't have to, really. I guess you could say it's more of a faith thing—something Levi and I are doing because we found this really great verse in the Psalms."

"Levi? I thought he was Amish."

"That's another story," I interrupted, not wanting to share Levi's plans just yet.

"So you're saying Levi's not into powwowing—that folk-healing thing some of the Amish farmers do?"

I'd heard about it, too. But most of the Amish I knew frowned on the practice. They viewed the use of charms, amulets, and silent incantations as questionable. Possibly evil.

I took Lissa into Susie's room. "Here she is," I said, introducing Lissa to my friend. "And, Susie, this is my girlfriend from school, Lissa Vyner."

"This is so weird, Mer. You're talking to Susie like she hears you." Lissa stared at me.

I nodded. "I honestly think she does."

"Really?"

"It's a strong feeling I have."

Lissa and I stood at the foot of Susie's bed and talked about all sorts of things. I couldn't believe how far behind I'd gotten on the activities at our church youth group.

"Don't forget we're having that river hike tomorrow," she reminded me. "Maybe you and I can team up."

"I'm sorry, but I can't go. My aunt and uncle are coming with their new twin babies."

"Lucky for you," she said pensively. Then, "I've really

missed you, Mer. It seems like ages since we've really talked."

"I know what you mean." I was curious about what had happened between her and Jon, but I didn't dare ask.

After she left, I pulled two chairs of equal height together, making a little bed for myself. When I had both chairs situated so I could stretch my legs out slightly, I positioned the pillows, then reached for the Bible.

Susie and I were going to have a Bible study. She was going to know what God's Word said about miracles.

I propped my pillows up so I could see her from my chair-bed. My plan was to talk until I fell asleep. Maybe I'd even talk *in* my sleep!

Long after midnight, the super-friendly nurse came in for a routine check. "Everyone ought to have a friend like you, Merry." Her words were the very last thing I remembered as I fell, exhausted, into a deep sleep.

❧   ❧

Sometime just before dawn, I awoke with a start. The Bible had slid off my lap, inching its way down against Susie's bed. The hard edge poked into my legs.

Drowsily, I reached for it, putting it on the table. Then I began the flow of words to Susie's brain. "It's almost morning, and can you believe it—I've been here all night! This is my very first hospital sleepover." I chuckled to myself. "Sleepovers are supposed to be full of excitement. People aren't *really* supposed to sleep at these things, you know. So, c'mon, Susie, won'tcha ple-ease wake up?" I stretched a bit, trying to get the kink out of my neck.

Then I felt it. Something powerful. My heart beat a little too fast, and I looked over my shoulder, wondering if an angel had come to call.

Rubbing my eyes, I heard a tiny sound. It came from Susie's bed. My arms froze in place as I turned around.

Slowly, I opened my eyes, half expecting to see her guardian angel.

"Wo bin ich?" came her husky voice. "Where am I?"

I sat up, nearly falling out of my makeshift bed of chairs.

SEVENTEEN

"Susie! You're back!"

I was afraid to hug her, but I leaned over the bed, smiling, not sure what to do.

"What happened?" she asked, sounding groggy.

"There was an accident. But you're going to be fine now."

"Come one, come all . . ." Her voice was weak.

I grinned down at her blue, blue eyes. "Susie . . . could you hear me reading to you? Did you—"

The door opened and the morning nurse breezed in. Her face burst into a surprised, but delighted, expression. "Well, what do you know!" She grinned from ear to ear, looking first at Susie, then at me.

"This is my friend, Susie Zook," I said.

From that moment on, there was a scurry of activity. Almost more than when Susie had been in the coma. Her Amish friends and relatives came from miles around to witness the truly amazing change in her.

"Jah, it's a miracle," Grandfather Zook said later, stroking his beard. He touched Susie's forehead lightly.

I noticed his hand tremble as he did.

"Well," he continued, "you shoulda seen them fireflies last night."

I explained to Susie that he'd brought a jarful to keep her company.

"Jah?" she said, eyes bright. "Ya brought 'um here? To the hospital?"

Grandfather nodded. "Right here, child." He showed her where the jar had sat on her chest, nearly touching her chin.

"Ya didn't let 'um die, didja?" she asked me.

I spoke up. "I set them free—right out in front of the hospital."

A smile spread across her thin face.

"And I read ya the last verse of my poem," Grandfather said. He didn't exactly sound proud, as in arrogant, but there *was* a hint of pleasure in his voice. "My work is done now, little one. My work is done."

His words gripped me. What did he mean?

"I wanna hear what you wrote, Grossdawdy," Susie said. "Can ya say it by heart?"

Grandfather reached into his black coat. "My mind's not what it used to be." He unfolded the paper, and I saw it shake as he began to read. " 'Tis the night of the fireflies, 'Tis the night of God's call. Dusk comes and is gone, and now . . . true light shines on us all."

Susie's face shone. "It's so-o pretty!"

He smiled. "It's *your* poem, child. 'Tis for you."

A soft, distant look crept into her eyes. "I had a dream about beautiful lights. Lights . . . everywhere."

I thought of the many Bible verses I'd read about God's light. Maybe Susie *had* heard my words.

Be strong and take courage. The words buzzed in my head as I left Susie's room. Filled with absolute delight, I headed down the hall to call my mother. In spite of the excitement, I knew I was worn out. My adrenaline was depleted; it was time to go home.

Susie would be coming home, too. Sooner than anyone ever expected.

ೞ   ೞ

"What a wonderful thing for you to witness first-hand," Mom said as she drove away from the hospital. She was cheerful and full of questions.

"I don't know how to explain it," I said. "Somehow I knew that I was supposed to be with Susie last night. And when she woke up . . . it was so-o incredible. It was the most wonderful thing that's ever happened to me."

"In your whole life?" Mom was smiling.

"In my whole, entire life!"

Mom was dressed up—her best white summer suit and pumps. I wondered if she was headed somewhere important. But when I asked her about it, she said she was celebrating life.

"Me too!" Actually, I couldn't wait to get home to SummerHill Lane. I needed a shower and a change of clothes. I'd been wearing the same clothes way too long.

Mom came into my bedroom to chat after I was dressed. Honestly, it was like old times. The tension between us had disappeared. She was relaxed about everything. Even when I told her Levi's plans to attend a Bible school. She didn't second-guess me the way she'd been doing the past few months.

"Guess we've all seen it coming," she said about Levi.

I cuddled both Abednego and Lily White. "For as long as I remember, he's been pushing the rules over there." I glanced out my bedroom window.

It was truly good to be home. The smell of the country and the sounds—it sure beat the hospital all to pieces!

"It's good to have you here, Merry," Mom said. The way she said it made me wonder. Had Susie's accident changed things for *everyone?*

❧   ❧

Susie came home on Saturday, the same day my aunt and uncle arrived with their six-week-old twins, my new cousins, Benjamin and Rebekah.

Miss Spindler showed up for the occasion. Her blue-gray kink of hair was all done up prissylike. "Oh, aren't they the most adorable little precious things ever!" she exclaimed when she saw the babies.

They were precious all right. Baby Benjamin wore the tiniest blue suit I'd ever seen. Petite Rebekah was dressed in one of Faithie's fanciest pink lace dresses—looking like a real live doll.

Mom took Rebekah from Aunt Teri, and Uncle Pete placed Benjamin in Miss Spindler's skinny arms. I stood back, observing Uncle Pete as he began signing rapidly for my deaf aunt's benefit. She broke into a big smile as Mom and Miss Spindler oohed and ahed over her darling babies.

I don't know why, but it took me several hours before I could get it together enough to hold them. I'd heard it was important to feel truly confident when holding an infant, and I certainly didn't feel that way now. Their teensy bodies, so fragile and delicate, could fall right through my fingers.

So for my first encounter with Ben and Becky, I sat on the living-room sofa and held them. One at a time.

I half expected my new baby cousins to cut loose crying when they sensed my uncertainty, but thank goodness, both of them slept right through their initial visit with me.

After lunch, I called Chelsea Davis to see if she was back from her Disneyland vacation. When Lissa Vyner answered, I was completely thrown off.

"Uh . . . is Chelsea there?"

"Oh, hi, Merry," Lissa said, recognizing my voice. "Just a sec."

Chelsea got right on the phone. "What's up, Mer?"

"How was California?" I asked.

"Hot, hot, and guess what?"

"You met a guy," I replied.

"How'd you know?"

"I have my ways," I said secretively.

"Well, how are you and Levi?" she asked.

"You won't believe everything that's happened." I filled her in on Susie's accident and miraculous recovery.

"Really? She pulled out of it, just like that?"

"Well, it wasn't really all that fast, I mean, she was out for almost *four* days."

"Man, I'd hate to think what I'd be missin' being stuck in the hospital that long," Chelsea said.

"Wouldn't we all," I whispered.

"By the way," she continued, "what's the deal with Jon Klein?"

"Better ask Lissa."

"She's not saying much. Are they—"

"Uh-huh."

"So does that mean you and—"

"Don't say anything! Promise me?" I said.

"Yeah, okay. But you better hurry and snag that boy before Ashley Horton does. I saw her eyeing him at the river hike today."

"*You* went on our church hike?" This was unbelievable!

"Now don't go getting all excited," she said.

It's a beginning, I thought, thrilled that my atheist friend had found her way to a church activity.

"Well, so what do you think?" she asked.

"About what?"

"About Ashley, your pastor's daughter? Does she have a chance with Jon or not?"

I honestly thought Ashley was a thing of the past. At least for Jon. "Probably not," I said.

Chelsea started laughing. "So . . . sounds to me like you're still interested in you-know-who?"

"Aw, Chelsea, for pete's sake." I groaned. "Is Lissa hearing all this?"

"She's in the kitchen raiding our cookie jar. Mom made brownies this morning."

"Bring some over," I teased.

"Maybe I will."

"Hey, you've gotta see my baby cousins," I said.

"Oh, so *now* you tell me!"

I peeked around the corner at the portable bassinets in the dining room. "They're sound asleep, but they'll be waking up soon to nurse. You should come see them before my aunt and uncle leave."

"Lissa, too?"

"Sure, that'd be great." I went on to explain that Lissa and I had made up last night at the hospital.

Chelsea was confused. "What was *she* doing there?"

"Trust me, it's fine."

I happened to glance out the window as I hung up the phone. Looked like a parade of buggies parked next door. Was there a work frolic going on?

Stepping out on the back steps, I strained my neck to see, but the willows blocked the Zook house from view. Still, the lineup of buggies and all the people made me wonder.

Surely, Rachel would've invited me if they were having something special for Susie. But it wasn't like the Amish to throw parties. Unless . . .

Fear clutched my throat. "Mom!" I raced inside.

Mom was sipping iced tea at the kitchen table with Uncle Pete. "Mom," I said, softly. "Can you come outside a sec?"

I guided her out to the backyard.

"Look." I pointed to the Zooks' front yard and their long, dirt lane. "Have you ever seen so many buggies?"

Mom frowned. "I hope Susie's all right."

"Me too!"

We both heard the phone ring, and Mom rushed inside to get it. In a few minutes, she was back outside, standing in the grass beside me. "Honey, that was Miss Spindler calling. She just saw the Amish funeral director drive away."

My hand flew to my mouth. "No! Not Susie!"

EIGHTEEN

I ran faster than ever before down SummerHill Lane and through the willow grove. Over the picket fence and into the meadow.

My heart pounded ninety miles an hour. *Susie . . . Susie . . . Susie.*

The Amish expected visitors to enter the house without knocking at a time like this. I caught my breath as I stepped through the front door and surveyed the large gathering of plain folk. The partition between the large living room and the kitchen had been removed, and relatives and friends were seated in a wide circle of somber faces.

Women scurried around in the kitchen, all of them dressed in black—washing dishes and busy with food preparations. Men were seated, silent and resigned. Only an occasional word was spoken by Abe Zook, who invited me to join the others.

Soon, Rachel came in and sat beside me on the wooden bench, briefly touching my hand. Her face was solemn and pale.

My throat was dry, too dry to speak. I coughed down

133

the tears. "What happened?" I whispered. "What went wrong?"

"He died in his sleep."

"*He?*"

"Grossdawdy," she said softly. "He sat down in his rocking chair after lunch and . . . was . . . gone."

I was overcome with emotion. Grandfather Zook? How could it be? He had come to the hospital last night . . . read his poem to Susie and . . . and . . .

Then I remembered his trembling hands. The way he'd said that his work was done.

My heart ached, remembering how I'd embraced the old gentleman. Overwhelmed, I let the news slowly soak in. Little Susie was alive . . . Jacob Zook was dead.

"He wanted to die at home," Rachel whispered. "If it was to be, it's best this way."

I nodded, my brain hazy. "How's Susie?"

"She's resting upstairs. Wanna see her?"

I nodded, and we tiptoed through the sitting room to the steep, wooden stairs. When we arrived in Susie's room, she glanced up from her bed.

A smile swept across her rosy-cheeked face. "When are we gonna catch fireflies again, Merry?"

I hurried to her and smoothed the handmade quilt at the foot of the maple bed. "As soon as you feel better."

"I'm gut, really I am," she insisted. "Mam wants me to rest up so I can go to Grossdawdy's funeral."

I looked at Rachel. "When will it be?"

"Monday." She folded her hands and stared at the floor.

Susie pleaded, "Oh, Merry, you must come."

"Sh-h!" Rachel warned. "Keep your voice down."

Susie nodded her head slowly, looking repentant.

Rachel moved across the uneven floor to a framed piece on the wall above the bed. Carefully, she took it off the nail and showed it to me.

It was the firefly poem, beautifully framed in solid pine. "Your grandfather made this?" I stroked the wood, feeling its silklike smoothness.

Rachel nodded. "After breakfast Grossdawdy was out in the barn hand-rubbing the wood."

I studied the poem, written in Jacob Zook's own hand. " 'Night of the Fireflies,' " I said thoughtfully. "He finished it just in time."

"Read the last verse to me," Susie said, leaning forward slightly.

I turned the framed poem so she could see it. Pointing to each word, I began, " 'Tis the night of the fireflies, 'Tis the night of God's call. Dusk comes and is gone, and now . . . True light shines on us all."

Tears filled Susie's eyes as she chanted the refrain. "Come one, come all, to the firefly ball . . ."

Suddenly, Rachel's face grew serious. "Ach! Grossdawdy must've known." She peered over my shoulder. "Look, it says, ' 'Tis the night of God's call.' "

It was hard to put into words, but looking at the last verse, it almost seemed that Grandfather Zook *had* known—that he was preparing us.

After a silent moment, Susie spoke. "I like this line best." She pointed to the last line. "True light shines on us all."

"Jah," Rachel whispered. "Jah."

❧   ❧

Three different clocks chimed nine times in the Zooks' house on Monday morning. When the last clock stopped, the Amish bishop removed his hat. At once, all the other Amishmen took off their straw hats in a swift, precise motion.

Benches had been placed parallel with the length of each of the three large rooms. The kitchen, dining room, and living room were packed with nearly two hundred and fifty people, as many as had attended Curly John and Sarah's wedding last November. They, along with the other Zook family members, sat facing the unpainted pine coffin at the end of the living room with their backs to the ministers.

I noticed Esther glance at Susie once during the thirty-minute *first* sermon. The speaker made reference to the fact that God had spoken to us through the death of a brother.

"We do not wish our brother Jacob back, but rather we shall prepare to follow after this departed one. His voice no longer is heard amongst us. His hand is absent at the plow; his presence—'tis no longer felt. His bed is empty, his chair . . ."

I tuned the minister out. Hearing the way these people accepted the death of this dear, dear man made me even sadder than his passing. Where were the words of comfort, the words describing his beautiful, joyous life? The joy, the love he'd passed to others? The way he loved God?

Fidgeting slightly, I wondered how Levi felt about all

this now. Was he feeling the pain, too?

A second minister stood to his feet and began to say that a call from heaven, a loud call, had come to this very assembly. "The holy Scriptures admonish each one of us to be ready to meet our death. We do not know when it is that our own time will come, but most importantly— we *must* be ready!"

I studied the steady rising and falling of Susie's, Aaron's, Ella Mae's, and Nancy's shoulders as they sat next to each other, looking like stairsteps. Rachel and Levi sat at the end of the bench row. Their bereaved grandmother sat between Abe and Esther, and, occasionally, she slumped in her chair. I held my breath, hoping she wouldn't pass out or maybe even pass away in front of our eyes.

Amish funerals usually lasted about two and a half hours. I felt truly sorry for Grandma Zook. Then, when the minister began to direct his comments toward the teenagers gathered there, I began to feel sorry for Levi.

"My dear young people," he said, "when you reach the age to think of joining the church, please do not put it off." The words were accented with strong emotion, and I wondered if they would have an impact on Levi and his plans for the future.

Two long passages from the Bible were read. But no one said anything about Jacob Zook's life. The thrust of the sermons was an appeal to the people to live godly, righteous lives. To prepare for death, as well.

Next, the first minister stood up and read a brief obituary. "Jacob's memory is a keepsake—with that we cannot part. His soul is in God's keeping. We have him in our hearts."

There were no flowers at this funeral. No music either. Someone read an Amish hymn, then all of us sitting in the living room went outside while the ministers arranged for the coffin to be placed on the front porch—the most convenient area for the final viewing.

Abe, Esther, Grandma Zook, and all the Zook children stood behind the open coffin as the long line of friends and relatives filed past. Some shed tears, but I didn't hear any weeping. Not even from Jacob's widow. It was surprising how matter-of-fact these dear friends were about embracing death.

I wondered if things would've been different if Susie had been the one lying in the pine box today. But it was Jacob's time, the minister had said. *Jacob's*.

When I stood in front of the coffin to say goodbye to Grandfather Zook, Susie left her family and tiptoed silently to stand beside me.

Gently, she slipped her little hand into mine and whispered, "Come one, come all, to the firefly ball. Dance with 'um, laugh with 'um. Run straight and tall."

Through my tears, I saw Grandfather Zook's body dressed in the traditional white—a special white burial vest and trousers. His white dress shirt was neatly pressed for the occasion.

I held in the sobs that threatened to burst out, remembering the feel of his face against my hand in the hospital—my arms around him. I remembered the exuberant way he'd read his poem that first night, here on the front porch while he sat in his hickory rocker. And the way he'd

brought the jar of fireflies to the hospital for his unconscious granddaughter.

"True light shines on us all," I whispered. "I'll miss
you, Grandfather."

Susie let go of my hand and slipped back into line with
her family. I walked to the driveway to stand with the rest
of the mourners, waiting for the horse and buggy pro-
cessional to the graveyard. I glanced over at a group of
Amish teen boys preparing the hearse—a one-horse
spring wagon with the seat pushed forward.

At last, the viewing line ended; the horses were
hitched up to the many buggies parked in the side yard
and along the Zooks' lane. Levi was going to drive one of
them since there wasn't room in the family buggy for all
the Zooks. So Rachel, Nancy, and Susie rode with Levi
and me.

What a long procession it was. Susie sat close to me
up front, sometimes leaning her head against my shoulder.

"How are you feeling?" I asked her.

"Not sick, just lonely."

For Grandfather, I thought as I watched the stately line
of horses and carriages slowly making their way down
SummerHill Lane. A sobering sight.

"There're about two hundred buggies in the caravan
today," Levi remarked, glancing at me. "It'll take us
about an hour. Hope you won't be too tired."

It was a thoughtful thing for him to say. After all, I
was used to getting places fast in our fancy cars. But today, the slowed pace allowed time for reflection. A nice
change from the hustle-bustle of the modern world.

By the time we arrived at the Amish cemetery, the sun was high overhead. Susie and Rachel stood on either side of me as four pallbearers carried the coffin to the appointed sight. The hole in the earth was ready, and Susie reached for my hand, squeezing it hard as her grandfather's coffin was lowered into the ground.

The pallbearers dug their shovels into the rich Pennsylvania soil. *Clump.* The sound of the dirt hitting the top of the coffin brought tears again to my eyes. Susie sniffled, and Rachel kept her hands tightly folded as she stared at the ground.

When the hole was half filled, one of the ministers read a hymn. Then another recited, "The Lord giveth; the Lord taketh away. . . ."

I glanced down at Susie, surprised to see an endearing smile on her angelic face. *The Lord giveth.*

How glad I was that the Lord had given her back—had answered my prayers. I wanted to sing for joy. I wanted to run around and shout God's mercies to the mourners. But I didn't want to embarrass Levi or Rachel, and I certainly didn't want to give my spunky little friend any ideas. However, I must admit, I was mighty thankful. God was good!

NINETEEN

Susie and I eventually did go chasing fireflies. Levi and Rachel got in on the fun, too. We taught them to say the poem by heart.

Word of Jacob Zook's poem spread up and down SummerHill. Everyone was saying it, and those who hadn't learned it wanted to.

I got the bright idea to self-publish it—even took some time-exposed shots with my camera at dusk one night. The sky was hazy red and the fireflies were dancing and twinkling everywhere you looked. One picture turned out better than the rest, so I made a bunch of copies to go along with the poem.

Rachel, Susie, and I had a regular assembly line going. Rachel copied the poem in her own handwriting, I glued the photo in place, and all three of us started distributing them.

Before long, every neighbor on SummerHill had a hand-printed copy of the poem with the picture glued to the bottom.

As for Lissa, she and I started spending more time together. Lots more. We secretly teamed up to pray for

Chelsea. When I told Levi, he wanted to be in on it, too. The way I see it, Chelsea doesn't stand a chance continuing her self-declared atheist routine.

Jon Klein called several times, and we actually started playing our alliteration game again. Maybe Ashley Horton *is* going to make her move, but I'm not worried. She can't alliterate worth beans!

Which brings me to Levi. My Amish friend wants to take his GED so he can go to Bible School in September. I'm excited for him, and if all goes well, he'll be a college freshman.

Freshman—now *that's* a scary word. Ninth grade's coming up mighty fast. Too fast. I guess if I could make a wish and have it come true, I'd want the summer to last forever.

Earlier tonight, Rachel, Susie, and I sat on their front porch sipping lemonade. In the stillness, I could almost hear Grandfather's sweet, wavering voice as though it were coming from his hickory rocker—now vacant in the fading light of dusk.

'Tis the night of the fireflies . . .

FROM BEVERLY ... TO YOU

❧   ❧

I'm delighted that you're reading SUMMERHILL SECRETS. Merry Hanson is such a fascinating character—I can't begin to count the times I laughed while writing her humorous scenes. And I must admit, I always cry with her.

Not so long ago, I was Merry's age, growing up in Lancaster County, the home of the Pennsylvania Dutch—my birthplace. My grandma Buchwalter was Mennonite, as were many of my mother's aunts, uncles, and cousins. Some of my school friends were also Mennonite, so my interest and appreciation for the "plain" folk began early.

It is they, the Mennonite and Amish people—farmers, carpenters, blacksmiths, shopkeepers, quiltmakers, teachers, schoolchildren, and bed and breakfast owners—who best assisted me with the research for this series. Even though I have kept their identity private, I am thankful for these wonderfully honest and helpful friends.

If you want to learn more about Rachel Zook and her people, ask for my Amish bibliography when you write. I'll send you the book list along with my latest newsletter. Please include a *self-addressed, stamped envelope* for all correspondence. Thanks!

Beverly Lewis
℅ Bethany House Publishers
11400 Hampshire Ave. S.
Minneapolis, MN 55438

Also by Beverly Lewis

PICTURE BOOKS

Annika's Secret Wish   Cows in the House

THE CUL-DE-SAC KIDS
Children's Fiction

The Double Dabble Surprise   Tarantula Toes
The Chicken Pox Panic   Green Gravy
The Crazy Christmas Angel Mystery   Backyard Bandit Mystery
No Grown-ups Allowed   Tree House Trouble
Frog Power   The Creepy Sleep-Over
The Mystery of Case D. Luc   The Great TV Turn-Off
The Stinky Sneakers Mystery   Piggy Party
Pickle Pizza   The Granny Game
Mailbox Mania   Mystery Mutt
The Mudhole Mystery   Big Bad Beans
Fiddlesticks   The Upside-Down Day
The Crabby Cat Caper   The Midnight Mystery

GIRLS ONLY (GO!)
Youth Fiction

Dreams on Ice   Reach for the Stars
Only the Best   Follow the Dream
A Perfect Match   Better Than Best
Photo Perfect

THE HERITAGE OF LANCASTER COUNTY

The Shunning   The Confession
The Reckoning

OTHER ADULT FICTION

The Postcard
The Crossroad
The Redemption of Sarah Cain
Sanctuary*
The Sunroom

*with David Lewis